P9-DMA-894

STILL LIVES

STILL LIVES

NATSUKI IKEZAWA

Translated by Dennis Keene

KODANSHA INTERNATIONAL
Tokyo • New York • London

ACKNOWLEDGMENT
The publisher wishes to thank Rengo Co., Ltd., a member of the
Association for 100 Japanese Books, for its contribution toward
the cost of publishing this translation.

"Ya Chaika" was first published in Japanese as "Yaa chaika" in
Chuokoron, March 1988, and in book form in *Suteiru raifu*,
Chuokoronsha, 1988.

"Uplink" was first published in Japanese as "Appurinku" in *Bungakkai*, March 1988, and in book form in *Mariko/Marikiita*,
Bungeishunju, 1990.

"Still Life" was first published in Japanese as "Suteiru raifu" in
Chuokoron, October 1987, and in book form in *Suteiru raifu*,
Chuokoronsha, 1988.

"Revenant" was first published in Japanese as "Kaette kita otoko"
in *Bungakkai*, April 1990, and in book form in *Mariko/Marikiita*,
Bungeishunju, 1990.

Distributed in the United States by Kodansha America, Inc., 114
Fifth Avenue, New York, N.Y. 10011, and in the United King-
dom and continental Europe by Kodansha Europe Ltd., 95 Ald-
wych, London WC2B 4JF. Published by Kodansha International
Ltd., 17-14 Otowa 1-chome, Bunkyo-ku, Tokyo 112, and Kodan-
sha America, Inc. Translation copyright © 1997 by Kodansha
International Ltd. All rights reserved. Printed in Japan.
First edition, 1997
97 98 99 00   10 9 8 7 6 5 4 3 2 1
ISBN 4-7700-2185-2

Ya Chaika   7

Uplink   81

Still Life   111

Revenant   169

YA CHAIKA

1

He started at the fruit and vegetables, wandered around the meat and fish, and picked out a few items from the dairy products and frozen food section. Then it was canned and bottled foods. Finally, after a trek to the back of the store for household goods, he topped off his load with tissues and toilet paper, and the cart was almost full.

"Haven't you got a bit much?" said Canna.

"Don't worry, I can pay for it."

"Don't be stupid. I'm not talking about money, am I?" she said, as if saying it to a school friend. She looked up at him. "There's still meat in the fridge, and you're coming back on Wednesday anyway, aren't you?"

"I certainly hope so. But I don't want you to starve to death while I'm away, do I?"

"You make me sound like a pet canary."

"And the more we buy now the less there'll be to carry when we go shopping next time."

"I suppose you know food is better when it's fresh?" she said cheekily.

"Which is a very good reason for eating it up quickly. You're a growing girl, you know."

"This is way too much for one person. And besides, I can't put on any weight now because it'll mess up my gym practice."

Still, Fumihiko was pleased that he'd bought so many groceries and other household things. Shopping often cheers people up, and at the moment he needed cheering.

He paid at the checkout and the two walked to the parking lot carrying their bags. It was muddy underfoot. Fumihiko thought how pointless it was to have shopping carts in the supermarket when you weren't allowed to take them into the parking lot; all you needed was someone outside to take charge of them once the customers were finished. But he didn't say this aloud because Canna would only point out that she'd heard it all umpteen times before. Always thinking of the same thing to complain about in the same situation was a sure sign of getting stuck in a routine.

"You feel sort of bad about it, don't you?" Canna said when they were in the car.

"What do you mean?"

"Leaving your daughter all by herself and going miles away on a business trip."

"Not a bit. But I do feel I have to leave her well provided for."

"I'll be all right. Think about it, Dad. You come back pretty late once or twice a week as it is, and it's not going to worry me if it happens two nights running. I'll eat my three meals a day and keep the place clean. And I'll also make sure they don't find out about it at school."

"I know that. I trust you. But it's two nights away this time, not just one, so, you know ..."

"Remember the first time you spent a night away? That wasn't so good. I mean, I ate my dinner and washed the dishes, locked and chained the door and turned off the gas, and then when you rang up I said I was fine, didn't I? Still, when I got into bed and suddenly realized I was all alone, I got so worked up I couldn't sleep."

"Were you frightened?"

"Not frightened exactly. Just sort of worked up because it was the middle of the night and everything. But it never bothered me after that. I got used to it. Maybe living by myself suits me."

"In that case you'd better learn to keep your room a bit tidier. Lazy people don't manage too well on their own."

"That's it, you see. It'd be nice to be on my own because I wouldn't have someone always bugging me about things like that."

The whole time they were getting the shopping out of the car, taking it up in the elevator and carrying it into the kitchen, Canna kept up her chatter. It seemed to Fumihiko that she was trying to say everything she wouldn't be able to say while he was gone. Then again, maybe she really didn't care if he went away. Maybe she enjoyed it, seeing it as a break in the daily routine. And maybe the fact that she made sure the school and the neighbors didn't know was simply because she liked being secretive.

"Are you leaving early tomorrow?"

"Yes, I have to. It's over four hundred miles. I want to get out of Tokyo before the rush starts."

"I'm practicing getting up early, so I'll be leaving home at six, about the same time as you, probably. You can drop me off at school."

"Very kind of you. But all right."

"Where are you going, anyway?"

"Far north. To the farthest part of Tohoku."

Canna didn't ask any more questions. He wasn't in the habit of giving her detailed information about his business trips. All she knew was that he spent half the week at work and the other half at home, and two or three times a year he went away on a longish trip. He had some problem with his ears that meant he couldn't travel by plane. A doctor who'd operated on them had said that any drop in pressure would induce stabbing pains. Normal atmospheric pressure changes were so gradual he didn't notice them, although he did think he tended to feel better on days when the pressure was high. But he couldn't bear taking elevators in tall buildings, and he used to joke that since he only felt comfortable at 1013 millibars, he didn't like to think what would happen to him in a plane if the cabin pressure suddenly dropped to around 750.

He never returned from these trips with presents for her, although he once brought home a whole tray of fresh fish he'd bought at a fishing port somewhere. What they couldn't eat themselves they had given to two or three neighbors they knew slightly. Canna did that. She hadn't told anybody at the time that she'd been left on her own. She didn't like people to feel sorry for her, and the idea of being invited to eat a fairly ordinary meal while being interrogated about her personal affairs she found frankly unattractive. Hardly anyone knew that her father went off on business trips, leaving her on her own. The fact that she was living alone with him was enough in itself to pique the curiosity of these idle housewives, who seemed to look on her as a prime candidate for sympathy. Canna's response was that if they had time to waste on things like that it was their way of life that was peculiar, not hers.

While they were eating dinner the phone rang. Canna answered it.

"Takatsu speaking ... Yes, he is ... Could you hold on a moment, please?"

She looked at Fumihiko and made a face.

"It's some fool who thinks I'm your wife. Name of Momoi."

Fumihiko took the receiver while Canna went on eating the stew and salad he'd prepared. The call lasted two or three minutes. He never spent long on the phone.

"That's done it," he said when he came back to the table. "The man I was going with has had an accident. I'll have to go by myself tomorrow."

"Will you be all right? It's a hell of a long way."

"I'll only be by myself as far as Sendai. I'll just have to keep taking breaks while I'm driving."

"Why not go by bullet train?"

"I don't feel like it. Apparently Momoi was injured playing golf. Got hit on the head by a flying ball. He had a concussion. The doctor took one look at the brain scan and said he'd better not drive for a while. He's still in the hospital anyway."

"Can't be helped, then," said Canna. "Still, the man who hit the ball must have been a pretty good shot."

"He's given *me* a headache, too."

"But you don't play golf yourself, do you, Dad?"

"I loathe it."

I keep a dinosaur as a pet.

There are a few things you have to be careful about if you keep a dinosaur. Dinosaurs are pretty big and they also have long necks, so their heads are very high above the ground. The trouble with keeping a pet like that in a normal house is that there aren't many opportunities to see its face close up; and if you can't see its expression you won't be able to take care of it properly. You won't be able to tell whether it's healthy or not or even what kind of mood it's in. By the time you notice that it's ill or really just sulking, it'll be too late and there'll be nothing you can do about it.

Luckily, my home is on the fifth floor of a large block of flats, and our balcony is exactly the same height as my dinosaur's face. I only have to remove the balcony railing and spread out some hay and he can stretch out his neck and eat it. Then I can get a good look at his face and stroke and pet him a bit. I call it stroking, but of course dinosaurs are very thick-skinned so what I actually do is pummel him on his muzzle. That really makes him happy.

The dinosaur I'm keeping is called a diplodocus. Nobody else around here has got one. There isn't enough room to keep a herd of them, so everyone has to make do with mine. I've heard that out in the country there are people keeping stegosauruses and triceratops. These particular dinosaurs are herbivores and not all that difficult to look after, but carnivores like the allosaurus and tyrannosaurus are impossible except in a place where there's a specialist somewhere near.

My diplodocus doesn't have a name. He's so big it wouldn't seem right to call him Spot or Pooh or Puff, so when I'm calling him or scolding him to his face I use his full name: Diplodocus. When I'm pounding him on his muzzle, though, I call him Dippy.

His nose tends to be cold when I feel it, but that doesn't mean he belongs to a cold-blooded species. After all, a dog's nose is cold, isn't it? Dippy sleeps most of the morning, usually till about ten o'clock. Some people might say that only proves he's a reptile because he can't move until the heat of the day has warmed him up, but I think he's just lazy and likes to sleep late. There are plenty of people like that.

When I get up in the morning I go out onto the balcony and look for him. We live on the outskirts of town and you can see across a large meadow to the woods beyond. Way off in the distance, you can make out the hazy outline of the hills, but Dippy would never go as far as that. Usually he's curled up asleep somewhere in the meadow, with his head tucked under his belly and his tail wrapped around him. If I can't see him anywhere, I get out my binoculars.

At about ten o'clock he starts to shake himself, then he stretches his neck and looks about him. It takes a bit longer for him to actually stand up. When you're as big as that it's quite a job getting from a horizontal to a vertical position. Dippy does it by using his tail as a support and gradually pushing with his feet until he's standing. He then nibbles a bit at the leaves of a nearby tree and waits until he's really wide awake. Because he weighs around ten tons, it's not surprising that when it rains the places where he's slept and pushed with his feet to get up turn into puddles. You can see these puddles all over the meadow in the rainy season. When the sun shines on them they sparkle beautifully.

Dippy always feels better when the sun shines. Again, some people will say that's because he's cold-blooded and his behavior is affected by the temperature of the air. All I can say to those people is: Don't you feel more cheerful and upbeat when it's a sunny day? Rainy days make everyone depressed.

At about twelve o'clock, Dippy starts lumbering toward my house. He likes most of the grass and leaves that grow in the meadow—eats practically anything, in fact—but at noon he knows that if he comes to my place he'll get some especially tasty hay. He's usually pretty punctual. As soon as I see him walking in this direction I take down the railing on the balcony, being careful not to fall off, then get twenty bundles of hay from inside and line them all up. According to his birth certificate he was born on Christmas Day, so he gets a special ration of thirty bundles of hay on that day. I doubt whether he knows the difference between twenty and thirty but, as far as I can tell, he always eats in a "merry" sort of way at Christmas.

Diplodocus is the slimmest of the dinosaurs, quite light in relation to his height, but even so he's an incredibly heavy animal. He does rather tend to plod, I know—lumbering slowly forward, heaving one foot in front of the other and swaying his long neck from side to side—yet he's actually going as fast as he can when he's heading for our balcony.

The people in our neighborhood all know that I'm keeping a

dinosaur, so nobody's crazy enough to park their car directly underneath the balcony. Just once, and that was quite a long time ago, a
visiting salesman who wasn't aware of the situation did leave his
car there a little before noon. Dippy was concentrating on his
lunch and not paying much attention to where he was walking, so
naturally he stepped on the car and squashed it flat. It was lucky
he didn't cut his foot on a piece of glass. I wonder if the salesman's company gave him a new car.

The special hay arrives once a week by truck. It has to be
imported from China and costs a fortune, but that's one thing
Daddy's quite generous about. The hay smells very nice, so nice I
once thought of using it in a salad, but it was tough and the salad
was terrible. The truck dumps the hay in front of our building and
it's my job to move between 140 and 150 bundles up to the fifth
floor in the elevator. It takes a good half hour to do this. I've told
the truck driver that he must make absolutely sure never to come
around noon. If a truckload arrived when Dippy was eating, he
would smell the new hay and turn around and probably eat it all
up in one go. Even if the truck drove off he'd probably go after it.
Dippy is never rough, it's true, but I think it would be a shame to
tempt him with a lot of food and then not let him eat it.

His droppings are collected once a month when the farming
co-op sends a truck and a loader for it. Since he eats plenty of grass
and leaves every day, it makes lovely fertilizer. The truck and the
loader go all around the meadow picking up the droppings and
then drive off. I'm often allowed to sit next to the driver and circle
the meadow with him. Dippy's dung smells good. He must be
pretty proud of himself producing sweet-smelling stuff like that.

I don't get any money from the sale of the dung; it all goes to
the business that owns the meadow. Dad says that in any case it's
doubtful I can legally be said to own Dippy; apparently I'm just
the person who gives him his feed, I don't actually own him—all

that great bulk and that cool character of his. But I'm not both-
ered—it's just nitpicking. All I know is that I'm the only person
allowed to bang Dippy on the nose.

If I had a body like a cat's that wouldn't get hurt falling from a
fifth-floor balcony, I would really like to go for a ride on Dippy's
head. I'd perch right on top and off we'd go across the meadow to
those distant hills. When you look at things from high up, they
become wonderfully clear and sharp. Dippy's head would sway a
lot, I suppose, and the scenery would sway too and I expect I'd get
dizzy. Still, I'd be the only girl in the world to have ridden on a
diplodocus.

One good thing about having a dinosaur for a pet is that they
live a long time. My Dippy's bound to live at least a hundred years.
When I'm a really old lady I'll still be feeding him his hay. When
that time comes and I can't afford the hay any more, I'll probably
have to commit a crime or something to pay for it. I wonder how
much they'd let a really old lady get away with.

The Tohoku expressway was easy driving. Once the road
turned due north, it was as if the terrain ahead were pulling the
car toward it. Every time Fumihiko left Tokyo, no matter what
direction he was headed in, he experienced a similar sensation;
but this road had so few hills and bends the feeling was unusually strong. Once outside the city proper, he'd taken the metropolitan expressway, which ran alongside a series of waterways
for a while, passed swiftly through a bleak urban landscape and
deposited him at last on a wide, green plain. From that point
on, the plain seemed to extend endlessly, with hardly a hill in
sight. He began to feel something close to exhilaration as he
drove.

He was glad he'd decided to go by car rather than train. The
idea of spending four hours sitting opposite some stranger, only

a yard apart, looking and being looked at, was not one to be relished. In a car on the expressway, the strangers were all thirty yards away and you didn't have to see their faces. Everyone kept their distance, only occasionally signaling their intentions with a blinking light. After continuing like this for a while, it was amazing to find, on entering a service area, how many living beings were actually on the road.

When he left Tokyo it had been raining heavily, but the rain stopped after Nasu, and by the time he pulled into the parking area at Abukuma for a short rest the sky had brightened. He felt an urge to call Canna and talk to her about the progress he was making. He imagined her making a game out of following his route on a map. She could find out the weather forecasts for the places he had to pass through, which would not only be helpful but would give her an idea of the size of the country and how the weather bureau that published the forecasts worked. He could even carry a thermometer and a barometer in the car with him, making the game genuinely educational for her. In any case, it would be a lot of fun for a father and daughter separated by all those miles.

But Canna wouldn't be at home. She'd be at school, learning about trigonometric functions, English participial constructions, the achievements of the first emperors and the meaning of the prologue to the Japanese Constitution. Or she'd be lending a sympathetic ear to some friend with a problem. Or passing a note around the class making fun of an incompetent teacher. Or eating chocolates. Whatever she was doing, when it was over it would be time for gym practice, since that seemed to be a more important part of her school life than her studies did. Practice was intense and went on for hours, from the time the gym was still lit by the hazy rays of the afternoon sun coming in through the high windows until the electric lights eclipsed the sun and it was quite dark outside. The girls all seemed proud of the sheer amount of time they spent working their bodies like lumps of clay.

Afterward, they would drop in for a snack somewhere on their way to the station, laughing at mindless jokes while they ate. This habit was just one more aspect of the day's session, a kind of mental gymnastics to finish up with. And when that was over, the girls would separate and head for home. Canna's supper would be a simple meal she ate alone in front of the television. Later she'd have a bath, do a little homework perhaps, then go to bed. Or else she'd phone somebody, talking late into the night. She always washed her hair in the morning. That was her day, her fixed routine.

After Abukuma, there were mountains directly ahead. The surrounding scenery was being reshuffled now with each succeeding curve in the road. Every bend he rounded and every hill he crested, he waited for something new to appear, but it remained the same succession of turns and dips and rises. Occasionally place names flashed out at him, but none of them meant anything; they were just roads branching off to the left, names linked to no landscape that he knew and matching nothing in his memory.

His physical movements and mental reactions were gradually becoming more and more mechanical, and he could sense his field of vision narrowing. He stayed in the middle lane, maintaining a steady sixty miles an hour and keeping a fixed distance from the vehicle in front of him. If the distance shortened, he made the decision either to slow down or overtake, programming his behavior as he watched the minutes tick by and noted each successive signpost that brought him closer to his goal. He had stopped feeling tired, since the only thing working in his head now was the driving program inserted there. When that got overloaded and he felt his mind blurring, he would pull into a service area, use the toilet, drink a paper cup of coffee and stretch his back. That was all part of the program too.

Entrusting one's body to a fixed routine inspires a kind of pleasure that people rarely notice. Or maybe they do notice it but lack the words to describe it adequately. It could be plowing a field, using the same motions over and over again; or walking behind a flock of sheep as they follow their leader, making sure they don't drift away or come within range of wolves or wild dogs; or it could simply be a matter of making one or two hundred identically shaped objects every day. By repeating the same actions continuously, you are teaching your body something. The pleasure comes from doing that—like Canna on the beam, on the mat, on the uneven parallel bars, on the vaulting horse.

In Sendai he was joined by two people from the service department of his company's branch office and was able to leave the driving to them after that. Toward evening they arrived at Misawa, where they spent the night. The next day, while the other two carried out routine maintenance work, he talked to the supervisor of the plant he was visiting about the performance of the machinery that had been supplied by his company. In the afternoon he gave a lecture on recent technological advances and future trends. He explained how the latest digital communication equipment was particularly resistant to noise and interference, citing the system in use on the unmanned space probe that had been sent to investigate the outer planets. He wrote the details on a blackboard. Enormous technological improvements had been required to send such quantities of information accurately across such huge distances—across literally billions of miles—and the effects of these improvements were now spreading across the whole field. He went on to give an account of his own specialty, the central computer that coordinated all the communication devices.

Fumihiko got back to his hotel at eleven and tried phoning Canna. She must have been asleep, because the phone rang seven times before she picked it up and answered in a sullen, abrupt voice. Yes, she was all right. No, nothing had happened. He felt stupid to have bothered her with his unnecessary worries. She hadn't upset a pot of boiling water and scalded herself; the school bus hadn't fallen over a cliff; she hadn't been assaulted by a thug on the street. He told himself that he was anxious only because he'd been programmed to behave that way, as the "worried father." If he didn't adjust his data to include the growth factor he was bound to get into trouble for treating Canna like a child. He wondered whether he should devise a whole new program for her, but even while he lay there thinking about the form it might take he dropped off into a drunken sleep.

Driving back the next day, he found that the road looked very different from when he'd come. He and his two companions had returned to Sendai, where he'd put in an appearance at the branch office, squeezing in lunch between two consultation sessions. By the time he had completed his business and got onto the expressway, it was already past two in the afternoon. Exhaustion began to seep through his body, but when he got to the Fukushima-Iizaka interchange he noted with disgust a sign saying he still had another hundred and fifty miles to go. To make matters worse, he seemed to have caught some kind of cold, because his head felt heavy, as if enveloped in a fog.

The red taillights ahead of him, swaying in the frame of the windshield, reminded him of one of those video games. Everything in his field of vision moved in response to his manipulation of the steering wheel and the pressure of his foot on the accelerator, swinging from right to left, then left to right, now receding, now approaching. The things he was looking at weren't real: behind that glass screen was nothing but a vacuum backed up by an integrated circuit and a few distributing wires. If he played badly, all that would happen would be the screen going blank, his score coming up in the middle of it, followed by the sign indicating that the game was over. The kind of accident where the car actually crashed into some hard object, with the shock of the impact being transmitted to his own body, was unimaginable. He couldn't believe that was an actual road outside. It had to be a booth he was playing in, designed to make it seem that way.

As he struggled with the illusion that he was only playing a game, he started to feel drowsy. His interest in the red lights on the screen faded and he no longer cared if he won the game or not. His vision seemed to have narrowed, too. This was getting a bit dangerous. Probably he should just take a rest. A sign announcing the turnoff to the next service area caught his attention. Adatara, one mile. He switched into the left-hand lane and slowed down. Even so, the unbroken white line marking the left side of the road was completely blurred. He was blinking much more frequently now.

Adatara was empty. A cold wind was blowing across the car park, and the shopping area was deserted. It was only early evening, but it felt like midnight. He sat in a corner of the restaurant and had some coffee. It was already dark outside; the ceiling lights made distant points in the huge plate-glass windows, long, symmetrical rows of them like the lights from a row of spaceships in the sky beyond. First one would take off, then another, smoothly slipping away toward the same far-off point. A pure vacuum lay beyond the glass—not the false vacuum that lies behind the video screen, but an endless, authentic nothingness.

Tokyo was still a long way off. He could only hope that the caffeine would have some effect. Then, just as he was feeling that his head had cleared a little and he was ready to go, someone approached his table and stopped in front of it.

"Ahem. Excuse me ...," a diffident voice said.

Fumihiko looked up, thinking it might be someone he knew. But the face of the solidly built foreigner who stood there was unfamiliar to him. The man went on in a measured, courteous voice:

"I have a small request to make."

Fumihiko's immediate reaction was suspicion. The man was probably selling something, one of those missionary types maybe, or even a con man. But that seemed unlikely in the case of a foreigner, though speaking clumsy Japanese could sometimes help. Still, he didn't look the type. The tweed suit and dark red tie suggested a businessman.

So he nodded briefly and the other man sat down across from him. He looked a good ten years older than Fumihiko, although he could conceivably have been around the same age. His Japanese wasn't at all hesitant, but quite fluent and precise. He had a round face with a bushy moustache, and his eyes turned down at the corners. He didn't look particularly European; if anything, he had a rather oriental look to him despite his ruddy complexion.

"I am afraid I'm in something of a predicament and wonder if you would be so kind as to give me some assistance."

There was something about the man's eyes as he spoke that gave the impression of suppressed amusement. His Japanese was certainly very good, though overly polite. He must have been the brightest student in his class, as well as the most cheerful.

"I'm sorry. I should have introduced myself. My card," he said.

He took a card holder out of his inside pocket and handed one over. Siberian Lumber Export Corporation: Japan Branch Representative, Pavel Ivanovich Khukin. Minato Ward, Tokyo. So he was a Russian.

"Is there something in particular you ...?"

"Yes, I am afraid my car has broken down ..."

"And?"

"Perhaps I should start from the beginning. What I am mainly involved with is the importing of lumber from the Soviet Union into this country. I am based in Tokyo, but yesterday I had business in Fukushima, and on my way back I had trouble with my car. They had a look at it in that garage" (he waved at some place beyond the darkened window) "but they are missing the relevant spare part and the car will not be ready until tomorrow. I have no objection to leaving my car with them, but I myself am obliged to get back to Tokyo today."

Fumihiko listened in silence. The impression of barely repressed laughter continued like an undercurrent throughout everything the man said. Perhaps that was just the way Russian was spoken, which meant that he must have spent forty or fifty years constantly restraining a natural tendency to smile.

"Consequently I have taken the liberty of approaching a total stranger to request that, if by chance you should be on your way to Tokyo, you would be so kind as to allow me to accompany you. I can assure you that I shall do my utmost to cause you no inconvenience whatsoever."

Fumihiko found himself listening less to what the man was saying than to the way he said it. That degree of fluency must have taken years of practice. His own command of English was practically nil by comparison.

He roused himself and considered the man's request.

"You're from Russia?" he asked rather pointlessly.

"Yes. I come from the Soviet Union."

"How long have you been in Japan?"

"It must be about ten years now. Yes, ten years."

Fumihiko thought how long ten years was. A whole decade spent polishing his Japanese to get it up to this standard! Just thinking of the effort involved made him feel momentarily exhausted, which reminded of his own situation and the distance he still had to drive back to Tokyo.

"All right, then," he said. "I'll give you a lift back to Tokyo, but on two conditions."

The man looked at him intently.

"The first is that you don't smoke. The second is that you drive. I'm feeling quite worn out already."

This time the Russian smiled openly, the corners of his eyes slanting more noticeably downward and the smile spreading wide.

"That really is most obliging of you. Both conditions are quite acceptable. I do not smoke and I am adept at driving. I have maintained a clean record ever since I came to Japan; no accidents, no traffic offenses."

They got up and went outside. On the far side of the large car park was a gasoline station that also carried out minor repairs.

"That is my car," said the Russian, pointing. A small blue car was parked at the side of the repair shop.

"It'll be fixed by tomorrow?"

"That is what they say. I will send one of my men to collect it."

Fumihiko's car wasn't an automatic, but the Russian, after trying the clutch a couple of times, slipped it easily into gear and set off. They merged smoothly with the traffic on the expressway.

After they had been driving long enough for the Russian to get the feel of the car, Fumihiko decided to start up a conversation, but found himself fumbling for the man's name.

"It's Khukin. Pavel Ivanovich Khukin."

He pronounced the name in precise syllables as a Japanese would, which meant he also knew the writing system.

"I imagine, Mr. Khukin, that people are always telling you how good your Japanese is."

"Well, I have been here for ten years, so it is not all that surprising. I also come from a town which had a Japanese language school before anywhere else in the world."

"Where's that?"

"Irkutsk. Have you heard of it?"

"I've got a fair idea where it is but, of course, I've never been there. Eastern Siberia, isn't it?"

"That is so. On the shore of Lake Baikal. Around the middle of the eighteenth century they already had a Japanese school. A Japanese castaway was the teacher."

Khukin explained that Lake Baikal was the same shape as the mainland of Japan, and the peninsula that extended into it was exactly the same size as Tokyo Bay.

"If we could transport it here we could reclaim Tokyo Bay perfectly," he said, and chuckled. From the way he said it he must have made the same remark many times before to various Japanese acquaintances.

"I wonder if you would mind telling me your name," he said after a moment.

"Oh, of course. I'm sorry. It's Fumihiko Takatsu."

"Mr. Takatsu."

They were silent for a while. Now that the Russian had introduced himself and covered the topics that naturally followed, he evidently had nothing in particular to say. Neither did

Fumihiko. The car ran smoothly on, and he was starting to feel sleepy. Khukin's driving was impeccable; he felt safe in his hands. It was warm in the car, too, and he had every reason to be tired. It was pleasant to lay one's head on the back rest and doze off. He wasn't sure if he'd started dreaming, but the images that floated up in his mind were vague, disconnected. It seemed to him that he sat suspended in this half-dreaming state for a long time, although that was probably an illusion.

When he finally opened his eyes, he remembered where he was and the presence of the Russian. He checked the view ahead. The taillights of the car in front looked blurred and those farther off seemed to be disappearing into a haze.

"It's fog," said Khukin, noting that he'd woken up.

"Unusual for this time of year," said Fumihiko, still not fully awake.

The fog writhed and swirled in the headlight beams. It still wasn't very thick. Khukin dropped his speed a little and Fumihiko showed him how to work the fog lights.

"I almost died in a fog once," Khukin said.

"When was that?" His head was almost clear now.

"When I was a boy. I was about ten years old. We often used to go skating. There were still many shortages then, unlike today, but on my previous birthday I had received a pair of skates. One of my father's men, a mechanic, had made them from the steel blade of a broken tractor. I was extremely proud of them."

"I used to skate, too," Fumihiko put in.

"Did you?" Khukin said, but went on with his own story. "We usually went to an artificial skating rink, but one Sunday I and two friends took our sandwiches and went by train two stations down the line to the River Angara. From that point to Lake Baikal the river is very wide, almost like a part of the lake itself.

And it was completely frozen over. The surface was much less even, of course, than the ice in the skating rink, and it was difficult to skate on, but it was so much fun to go zooming between the bumps. And then there was so much space to move in, which was a real pleasure. It was a beautiful, clear day, and I could skate to my heart's content.

"There was a railway station on the bank with a tall chimney beside it. You could discern it immediately, even from a distance. I felt it would be all right to skate quite a way out from the bank, because I could always guide myself back by the chimney, so I kept on going, farther and farther. My two friends remained near the bank since they were practicing ice hockey with some broken sticks and a piece of wood. So I kept on going, sometimes looking back to make sure I could still see the chimney, and each time it was a hundred yards farther off I felt this strange mixture of pride at what I was doing and anxiety because of the danger."

That's the way everyone feels when they go far from a fixed point of safety, thought Fumihiko, although there was something else about the story, too, that struck him as vaguely familiar.

"Eventually the chimney appeared no bigger than a matchstick. I decided I really had gone too far and began to think about going back. Nevertheless, I was feeling very pleased with myself. I wished I could leave some sign proving that I had come all this way.

"As soon as I set off back I noticed something white flowing toward me from the frozen surface of the lake. It was fog. I looked up and saw that the sky was still blue, but a cold shiver ran down my spine. In the town, the fog often came in so fast you lost sight of everything almost immediately. I knew I had to return to the chimney as quickly as possible. But the fog grew thicker, and now the chimney and all the buildings on the shore were hidden. I went as fast as I could in the direction where I had last seen the chimney. I knew I had to go in an absolutely straight line and that if I did not deviate from it at all I was bound to arrive at the railway station.

"The air I was breathing seemed pure white. When I looked up the sky was still blue, because the fog only extended thirty or forty feet above the surface of the ice. That meant I should have been able to see hills by now, and the large buildings and the chimney that were higher than the hills, but I could see nothing, just a brilliant sun shining on that white world. I began to panic."

Khukin was telling the story with genuine skill. He paused a while to let the suspense build, while Fumihiko waited for him to continue.

"I was still speeding along in what I considered to be the right direction when I suddenly fell over. I must have tripped on some bump in the ice and went head over heels, cutting the corner of my eye on the ice. There was a little bloodstain on the ice, but I did not feel any pain. In fact, I could not tell if it was just cold around my eye or actually hurting, and the blood soon stopped. The real trouble now was that the fall had made me lose my sense of direction.

"I just stood there and peered about me. I could not see a thing. Everything was white; not a thing was a visible. I wondered whether I could find the tracks of my skates, so I crawled about looking for them, but all I could see were natural indentations and cracks in the ice, not the sharp lines the edges of my skates would have cut. The sky was still blue directly above, but at fifty degrees north it gets dark early, even in spring. If the fog did not lift before nightfall I would freeze to death. It was a truly terrifying situation."

In the real world visible through the windshield the fog was gradually thickening, a swaying yellow wall in the fog lights. Khukin slowed down even more, following the dim taillights of the car ahead. Fumihiko went on listening to the story in silence.

"I tried calling out as loudly as I could, straining my ears for a reply, but not a sound could be heard. It seemed to me that even the loudest shout I could manage would be inaudible a mere five yards away. So I set out again in what I thought to be the direction of the chimney, but after only a few yards I became completely unsure of myself and stopped. Every direction looked the same and I could not tell which way was which. I was paralyzed.

"Because I was not moving, the tips of my fingers and toes were starting to tingle with the cold, but I had no idea what to do so I simply sat down where I was: Perhaps I wept a little. Afterward I realized I had sat there for only ten minutes at the most, but at the time it felt like three hours. The fog gave no sign of lifting. I could hear no one's voice."

"But you were rescued, of course," Fumihiko interrupted.

"That was indeed how it ended," said Khukin, resuming his normal tone. He even sounded a little regretful at being brought back so abruptly from Irkutsk to the inside of this car in distant Japan. Fumihiko felt that he'd said exactly the wrong thing.

"I was rescued by a dog," Khukin said.

"A dog?"

"Yes. While I was sitting on the ice without the slightest idea of what I should do, a large dog suddenly appeared out of the fog, a powerful-looking brown dog with shaggy hair and a short nose. This dog looked at me, snorted in a contemptuous sort of way, then bounded off again in the direction it had come from. Of course I set off after it. The dog ran without any hesitation, just looking back at me occasionally to make sure I was still following. It ran pretty fast but I was able to keep up all right because I was on skates. Then after we had gone quite a distance I realized I was only a hundred yards or so from the shore. Presumably because of the difference in temperature, the fog was confined to the ice. So I was able to make my way back to the railway station. The dog itself disappeared at some point."

"The fog's lifted here as well," said Fumihiko, noticing that the wisps of cloud clinging to the road had vanished and even distant taillights could be seen clearly.

"What about the dog?"

"I know nothing at all. Perhaps it was just wandering about in the fog, or perhaps its loyal instincts directed it to save a child. After I had rested a bit, I walked up and down the shore looking for it, but that dog was nowhere to be seen. I never saw it again. In fact this is the first time I have ever told this story to anybody."

"Anybody?"

"Yes. If I had told my parents they would have been angry with me. I did tell my two friends, but they did not believe me. They said I had just gone a little way into the fog, then made up a big story about it because I was such a baby. So after that I told nobody."

"Well, I believe you," said Fumihiko. "Although I think you were incredibly lucky."

"I think so myself."

They didn't say much after that. Khukin, apparently satisfied with the effect of his dramatic tale, was content to drive in silence. Fumihiko was thinking that Siberia might be an interesting place to visit when he fell asleep again.

By around 7:30, they were on the metropolitan expressway and shortly afterward he dropped Khukin near his office in the center of the city. Khukin asked for a card, which Fumihiko gave him.

"Thank you very much. I trust we shall meet again," Khukin said, then disappeared inside a large building. Fumihiko assumed he would never see him again.

"But what's so special about that story?" asked Canna, with a serious expression on her face.

"It's not the story, it's just that virtually the same thing happened to me once."

"You mean you nearly died when you were skating?"

"Well, I suppose it didn't really come close to that, because it was only on Lake Suwa. But here's what happened. When I was still at primary school I used to go to an indoor skating rink every Sunday and I was pretty good at it. Then your great-aunt Sachiko—you remember her?—well, she was going to Suwa and said she'd take me with her. It wasn't the winter vacation, though, come to think of it, so I wonder how I was able to go. Maybe the school was closed because of the flu or something. Anyway, we went to Lake Suwa, and I was enjoying myself skating around on the lake, since it was a weekday and there were no other kids about, when the fog came down. I was a city boy and had hardly ever seen real fog, so I thought it was great fun skating around and not being able to see where I was going. Until I finally realized I didn't know which direction the shore was."

"And then a great big dog came to rescue you?"

"No. There was no dog. It would have been nice to be able to say one of the sacred foxes from Suwa Shrine did it, but what actually saved me was the smell of curry."

"A plate of curry rice came bounding toward you, wagging its tail?"

"No, dear. Plates don't bound. I caught this whiff of curry.

Somebody must have been cooking in one of the lakeside houses. So my moment of panic was over. I figured out that if I could smell curry it meant the wind was blowing from the nearby shore. Then I remembered that the fog had come in from that direction. It wasn't much of a wind, but I decided to skate slowly against the way the fog was moving. After about two hundred yards, I could see the shore."

"The two stories really are alike, aren't they? Did you tell anyone about what happened to you?"

"No, not as far as I remember. In fact I'd completely forgotten about it myself. But while Khukin was talking I thought it was a strange coincidence, although I didn't mention it to him either. Still, he was a bit strange himself. Hitching a ride with someone and then suddenly coming out with a tale like that. I wonder if all Russians are that way?"

"I wish I could have met him too."

"Well, I suppose we might meet again some day."

2

I've only been to my father's office once, when I was in fifth grade at elementary school. My mother was still living with us then. She'd had a job selling jewelry for a few years, but right around that time she opened her own shop and became very busy with the accounts and other stuff. She always came home very late. Dad used to go to work three times a week, the way he does now, and spend the rest of the time working at home. The small computer he had at home was linked to the big one at the office, so there was no need for him to go in every day.

One day, I'm pretty sure it was the Monday after parents day at school, he said he had to go to the office but it would only be for an hour and he'd take me with him. We could go and see a movie when he'd finished. Of course I was thrilled.

The question was, what was I going to do for the hour while Dad was working? He thought a bit, then took me into a long room with a high ceiling. In one corner was a computer as big as a desk. There were electric wires all over the floor, and right in the middle a large box or case, about ten feet square, made of thick, transparent plastic. Some people in white coats were standing around it.

Dad went up to one of them and said something to him. I suppose he was asking him to look after me.

"Wait for me here," he told me. "You can watch the experiment they're doing in that box, but you mustn't tell anyone else about it."

I didn't know if he was being serious or making fun of me, so I just nodded.

Daddy went away. I sat on one of the chairs in front of the box and watched what was going on. Three things that looked like microphones had been set up on one of the inside walls. Wires were sticking out of them. On the floor in a corner there was a very complicated-looking machine which had a narrow pipe coming out of it. It looked like some sort of gun. There was nothing else inside the box.

The people in white coats took no notice of me but just went on checking the wiring and the programming system (Daddy used words like that when he was working at home, so I knew them) until, after quite a while, one of them said, "Okay, let's go."

The same man went and got a small bottle that was in the corner, then opened a tiny window in the box. Another man standing by the computer said, "Right."

The man with the bottle opened the cap very carefully, then pressed the mouth of the bottle flat against the opening. Little black things that had been inside the bottle flew into the box. They were flies, dozens of them. First they all flew together in a black swarm, but they soon broke up and flew about on their own. Then the gun-like machine in the corner started swiveling about with little jerks, aiming at one of the flies. It tracked this fly for a bit and then fired something like a needle at it. When it hit, the fly dropped down. It was just like people shooting birds, only there was no noise and nobody seemed to be doing it. The machine went on shooting down the flies and in a few minutes not one of them was left.

It was really interesting to watch. I figured out that the three things on the wall that looked like microphones tracked the flies for the computer, so the computer could tell the gun where to shoot. It must have been tough telling one fly from another with so many of them in there. Also, they flew about in such a higgledy-piggledy way that the computer had to have been really smart to target them so well. I felt sorry for the flies because there was absolutely no way they could escape.

This was repeated three times. I kept my eyes glued on the box. Each time the same thing happened. First the machine shot the ones that flew close to it; they were easy to hit and didn't last long. The ones further off took much longer, and the machine hesitated a lot before firing the needle. Just once a needle missed. The machine waited a bit, then fired another one and this time it scored a bull's-eye.

The third time was the last experiment for the day. Everybody gathered around the computer, discussing things as they looked at the printout. One of them opened a door into the box and went in and swept up the dead flies, then came over to me with the brush and pan still in his hand. I could see the flies had all been stabbed through with a thin dart about the size of a sewing needle. Some of them were still moving.

"Did you enjoy it?" the man said. He was young and quite good-looking.

"Yes," I said. Then, not knowing quite what I was supposed to say, I asked: "You don't kill butterflies, do you?"

"Butterflies don't make any noise when they fly, so they can't be tracked. Wasps would be all right, but they cost too much."

"Are flies cheap?"

"They're bred specially for researchers and zoos. There's lots of ways they can be used. Food for chameleons, for example."

I nodded. I wondered if a fly was better off being shot with a needle or eaten by a chameleon.

Then Dad came back and we went to a movie. On the train going home, I remembered the flies.

"Is it difficult to make a machine like that?"

"It certainly was in the early stages. The three mikes show where the flies are, but the hard part is picking out just one fly and predicting where it'll be a second later. If all you had was one stationary fly, anyone could hit it. Still, that machine was perfected three years ago; it's just being used for research purposes now. That's why I let you see it."

"What's it for, then?"

"It's supposed to be a demonstration device for auto-control anti-aircraft systems. The dart is shot by something like an air gun."

"I feel sorry for the flies."

"Well, the whole thing is a bit one-sided, I admit. The flies have got no missiles, or machine guns or bombs, or any anti-missile defenses either. There's been talk about arming them in the future, though."

"Seriously?"

"No, I'm just joking. Of course, that machine itself is a bit of a joke. It's only a computerized toy. No matter how big you made it, there's nothing it could be used for."

Dad had a funny, cynical sort of expression on his face when he said that. I'd never seen him look like that at home.

A few days after getting back from Tohoku, Fumihiko found himself still thinking about Siberia; obviously the Russian's story had made a surprisingly deep impression on him. Sometimes when he was working, or just sitting doing nothing, he found images appearing of things unknown to him in person: vast, white, snow-covered plains; mile upon mile of pine forests; a wide, frozen river; a small, dark town full of people on horse-drawn sleighs, bundled up in thick overcoats. Naturally he'd never been to Siberia, nor could he remember having seen any such scenes recently in a film or in a book of photographs. Perhaps they were just a product of pure imagination—he didn't know. All he knew was that his mind kept generating pictures of that huge, cold land while he stared out the window of his commuter train at a landscape he no longer saw, or while he was cooking a simple dinner and waiting for Canna to come home, or during that brief lull in the morning when he'd opened his eyes but not yet got out of bed.

A little horse was pulling a sleigh. White steam escaped from its nostrils, and its face was coated in perfectly white ice. A man was riding in the sleigh. He held the reins slackly, but the horse plodded on resolutely, as if it knew the road and was confident that home was not far off. Perhaps the man in the sleigh had fallen asleep.

A low sun hung above the horizon. Its rays gave no warmth, shining through the branches of pine trees, throwing long, beautiful silhouettes. The tips of the branches glittered and sparkled with ice. Beneath them passed a train, puffing out clouds of steam as it hauled a long, long line of cars, making the earth shudder as it rumbled by. The sun was a white disk peering through thin cloud. The clouds to the south spread out in a single fine sheet, but the sky above was brooding and heavy. The low, translucent sun would set in just two hours, but afterward, through the long hours of darkness, the night's light would be reflected off the snow and in its pale glow the vague shapes of things would still be visible. There was no wind, so it wasn't too cold.

Fumihiko assumed that some of these details in his mental picture must be wrong, knowing it was a landscape he had never seen. Maybe the sun was warmer than he thought; maybe the train didn't puff out clouds of steam and passed more quickly and silently; maybe nobody had horse-drawn sleighs any more, even in Siberia, and people stayed indoors all winter, hibernating like bears. Once these thoughts had surfaced, the horse-drawn sleighs and steam engine vanished from his head, but only after he'd enjoyed visualizing them several times.

So Fumihiko was not surprised when the Russian called him one day; in fact he answered as if he'd half expected it. No doubt a part of his mind wanted to know more about this distant world that had stirred his imagination so suddenly and deeply. The phone rang late one afternoon when he'd finally finished the review of a major project that had kept him cooped up in the house for three days.

"Hello. This is Khukin, the man you so kindly gave a lift to in your car the other day."

The voice was so friendly Fumihiko recalled the face instantly, with its characteristic expression of trying not to break into a smile.

"Ah, hello. Did you get your car fixed all right?"

"Of course. It came back in good shape the next day."

Khukin was inviting him out to dinner as a way of thanking him for his help. He wanted to take him to eat Russian food.

"Would you mind if I brought my daughter along as well?" Fumihiko asked on the spur of the moment.

"I should be delighted. How about your wife?"

"No, just my daughter."

Khukin didn't inquire any further, merely naming the time and place before hanging up.

When Canna got home from school and heard the news she was delighted. Probably excited by the prospect of meeting a real Russian, Fumihiko thought. On the afternoon of the appointed day, she took more time than usual choosing what to wear, saying she wanted to look as Russian as possible, though when she was ready Fumihiko didn't think she looked even remotely Russian.

"Well, well, Mr. Takatsu," said Khukin, when he met them outside the restaurant, "I had no idea you had so grown-up, so charmante, a daughter."

He looked amazingly cheerful, as if all the smiles he was in the habit of repressing had suddenly joined forces and taken over his face. Canna didn't look unhappy herself.

The food came in generous helpings and tasted rich but good. Khukin must have been a regular here, to judge by the banter he kept up with the attractively plump hostess. The restaurant was hot and Canna found herself playing with the large plateful of food in front of her.

"Come on, you must eat up," said Khukin. "You are a little on the thin side."

"Well, Comaneci and Nellie Kim are pretty thin, too."

"Ah, I see. You are also a gymnast?"

"Well, a bit."

This news seemed to please Khukin enormously.

"Then why do you not go to Russia to learn? We have many fine coaches. I will recommend you."

"Oh, I'm not at that kind of level."

"Then you must practice hard and get up to that level quickly. I will spare no efforts on your behalf, utilizing the most powerful connections and writing endless testimonials. I will make all the arrangements. Lodgings will be prepared for you in the Kremlin itself!"

"Well, let's see how it goes," said Canna, smiling modestly. Fumiko was puzzled, wondering why she was so unlike her normal self.

"Canna's always been an odd sort of child," he told their host. "Whenever she had a spare moment she used to stand on her head. Even if we were just waiting at the bus stop, she'd refuse to stand there in the usual fashion—suddenly she'd be upside down. I only had to take my eyes off her for a moment and she'd be climbing up the nearest tree or telegraph pole. The first time she saw a horizontal bar she thought it was something for practicing tightrope-walking on. When she found out what it's actually used for she wouldn't stop until she wore the skin off her hands. She's had five broken bones, and cuts and grazes happen all the time. I sometimes think she's walking proof of the theory of evolution."

"The theory of what?"

"Evolution. Darwin's idea that we're descended from apes."

"Ah, *evolutsiya*," Khukin said, smiling.

Canna had been looking down shyly, but now raised her head and said:

"Mr. Khukin, your Japanese is so incredibly good, I wonder if you know what this means: 'back flip with forward extended open leg somersault high bar dangle with forward fling'?"

"Well, that *is* a mouthful, indeed. What on earth is it?"

"It's what's they call the Comaneci somersault. It's a technique used on the uneven parallel bars."

"And can you do it, Miss Canna?"

"No way. I can only say it. Here's an even longer one: 'reverse open leg flat sole support flip forward turn with half twist backward extended somersault.' The Comaneci finish, for short. It's used to finish off a program on the balance beam."

"When you learn how to do it you must show me, please."

Fumihiko went on to ask Khukin about life in Irkutsk. Delighted, he talked with scarcely a pause for breath about his childhood, the local customs, winter and spring, trains, trams, buses, horses and carts, horse-drawn sleighs and a drink called kvass which vendors used to bring around in summer, winding up with a description of the extreme north of Siberia, the region of legendary cold. Fumihiko was surprised at how accurate his daydreams had been.

After that, it was Khukin's turn to listen with rapt attention to Fumihiko's account of his experience on Lake Suwa.

"Thus we have had almost the very same experience on the ice, and that is the reason we have become such firm friends."

The hackneyed phrase sounded oddly fresh when Khukin said it.

"Come to think of it," said Fumihiko, "in the not too distant past, Russia was thought of as our closest neighbor. Everybody sang Russian folk songs, and students were always going on about Dos and Tol."

"That is so. And then at some point Russia turned into a big, bad bear."

"What's Dos and Tol?" whispered Canna.

"Dostoevsky and Tolstoy," her father told her, adding: "You know, I've just remembered a curious thing. When I was a child I wrote a fan letter to Tereshkova."

"Who's Tereshkova? A film star?"

"A cosmonaut," said Khukin.

"The first woman in the world to go into space. I thought she must be an absolutely wonderful person, so I wrote her a letter. The first and only fan letter I ever wrote."

"Did you mail it?"

"No. I felt a bit silly about it. Also I didn't know her address."

Khukin laughed, a boisterous laugh that made the table shake.

"You Japanese people are incorrigible. She must have received hundreds of fan letters from all over the world, yet I am quite sure only a very few came from Japan. Many people here wrote her letters, but they all felt a little silly or shy, so they did not send them. As far as the address is concerned, the Russian embassy would do. Come, it is still not too late—hurry up and mail it."

"I'm afraid I mislaid it a long time ago. Also she doesn't go into space any more herself."

"No, she is in public relations now."

"'Ya chaika' is what she said, wasn't it?"

"Yes. You have remembered very well."

"What's that?"

"'Ya chaika': 'This is Seagull.' It was Valentina Tereshkova's call sign. They were the first words she transmitted back to earth after she'd gone into orbit."

"We all gathered around our radios and listened enraptured to those words. But I must say I preferred Yuri Gagarin to her. I was crazy about him. He was such a hero. Do you know what his call sign was?"

"No, I'm afraid I don't."

"'Ya oryol': 'This is Eagle.' A powerful, soaring eagle. But he died in a plane crash in 1968."

"Did he?"

Canna commented: "I suppose an eagle couldn't be like a

seagull, which only flies a bit and then takes it easy. He had to go on and on, trying too hard."

"That may well be so," said Khukin. "But we *wanted* a bird that would fly on and on. And Gagarin knew that."

"By 'we' do you mean the Russian people as a whole?"

"No. I am referring to small boys. When you are grown up you do not need heroes any more. That is how it goes."

As he heard this comment, Fumihiko found himself wondering what sort of hero Canna needed. To his surprise, he couldn't think of a single person who might qualify.

Lying in bed that night looking at the ceiling, Fumihiko tried to remember what he could possibly have written to Valentina Tereshkova. Had it been the kind of thing you could describe as a fan letter? He'd been fifteen at the time, and he knew he hadn't gone on about how wonderful he thought she was, and how brave, and how much he would like to meet her, and how he wanted to be a cosmonaut himself when he grew up. If that was all he'd felt, he would never have taken it into his head to write in the first place, nor would he have written so passionately and at such length and with so many revisions, slipping the perfected version into its envelope with the feeling that his soul had finally been released from something little short of possession. Nor would he have stuck it in the back of a drawer in his desk and forgotten about it for twenty-five years. He had told Khukin he'd felt too embarrassed to mail it, but that wasn't true. The truth was that once he had finally written it there was no longer any need to mail it. It wasn't as if he'd been anxious to get the autograph of the first woman cosmonaut in space.

Tereshkova circled the earth forty-eight times. The flight lasted seventy-one hours, taking her far above the blue sky and into the black night, where among the countless stars shining steadily in the dark vault of heaven the sun was just a singularly brilliant star and the moon a very big one. From that great height she had looked down on the earth, and the earth was green and blue and white, wrapped in a wispy layer of cloud, floating in a soundless universe, maintaining its slow, regular rotation beneath her eyes. She herself was rotating in another direction, so that it seemed as if she were drawing a fine thread diagonally, smoothly, around and around the earth; and the earth became a ball, wound about with the forty-eight multi-colored threads drawn by her orbits. What fired Fumihiko's imagination at the time was simply the thought of that gaze of hers, the idea that from this new star that had flown up to join the stars in heaven she was looking down, her gaze quietly enfolding every feature, every aspect, of the earth. This is what he'd wanted to convey to her when she came down: the fact that he'd felt her gaze upon them. The earth had been covered with a veil woven on the shuttle of her spacecraft's orbits, and this fragile web had adorned the planet more beautifully than the warm and cold currents of the oceans, the paths of the monsoon winds, the patterns made by stratus clouds, the aurora borealis or the Van Allen radiation belts. He had seen that cloth woven in the night sky. He had felt her eyes above looking down.

It wouldn't have been the same if it had been Gagarin up there gazing at the earth from that great height. Nor would Titov or Nikolayev or Popovich or Bykovsky have been right. It had to be a woman. When a man climbs into the sky he merely becomes more manly, the hero worshiped by the small boy Khukin. But when the woman Tereshkova rose up inside Vostok 6, she ceased to be a woman and became, not a man, but a point in space that was neither man nor woman, a point releasing that mysterious gaze, an eye that celebrated and blessed the earth it beheld, freeing us from the inadequate notion that God must be a man. This was not the eye of a stern God who judged, but the eye of a gentle angel who only watched and blessed, softly wrapping the earth in her ritual circlings.

That epiphany would never happen again. As Khukin had said, Tereshkova had come down to earth and stayed there. When Svetlana Savitskaya went into space, when Sally Ride went into space, they had been mere news items to him, events without significance. Space was no longer the realm of angels. By then Fumihiko himself had forgotten his earlier feelings, those obscure sensations that were so hard to put into words, the fleeting yet powerful emotions of that single night when he'd looked up into the sky, just as he'd forgotten the days of struggling to put it all on paper.

What made him feel now the way he used to feel about Tereshkova, overwhelmed by the sense of distant, unknown things, was the unmanned space probe that had left earth some years ago to visit the outer planets, one by one. He would lie awake listening to the quiet rise and fall of Canna's breathing as she slept in the adjoining room and think about this spacecraft that had already flown so far away it could be seen in the sky only as a tiny star, tinier even than Venus.

There it floated in cold, dark space, where there was no such thing as direction, no backward or forward, right or left, or even up or down, forbidden to seek shelter in the gravitational fields of bodies bigger than itself, flying in perfect solitude, at high speed, with never a sound or a vibration. Ahead and to one side of it there shone a star. In three years' time the probe would pass close to that star; but it wouldn't land there, just travel past, its course altered and accelerated by the star's gravitational pull so as to aim it at some more distant body. Finally it would leave the solar system, flying on into even emptier space, toward ever farther and colder stars. It would fly on for tens of thousands of years until eventually it crashed into some star-like body. If it were somehow capable of feeling awed by those vast distances, then it was going to have to feel awed for tens of thousands of years.

Sometimes greetings would arrive from earth, electric pulses that had traveled two hours through space to reach the probe's eagerly listening antenna. Whenever the craft approached a star, the messages from earth would become urgent, but where it was flying now the greetings were perfunctory: "Hello" or "Hi" would be about the extent of it. In reply, the space probe would report, "I'm getting on fine" or "I'm transmitting data about my general state of health" or "I just saw something interesting" or "I'm lonely," sending the messages on their two-hour return journey at tens of thousands of binary digits a second.

How would it feel to know you'd never return to earth? Obviously, reason told one that no mechanical device could feel anything. Only human beings looked up at the sky, narrowing their eyes and speculating earnestly about whatever gulf the probe might be traversing now, projecting their illusory emotions onto it. Human beings had trained this thing, supplied it with sources of energy, patted it on the back and sent it out into space. Then they stood around wondering what it was thinking out there in the midst of nothing and nobody, excited by its responses to those rare occasions when its master's voice was heard from far away.

Fumihiko knew that emotions didn't exist in space, yet he was also aware that his own perception of the machine was constantly fluctuating: one minute he saw it in human terms, the next as a purely mechanical object. The truth was that many people felt an emotional connection with a space probe which itself felt nothing. Every once in a while they remembered its existence and briefly tried to imagine, with the help of the TV camera that was its eyes and memory, what view of the universe it might be enjoying now, its excitement as it drew closer to its next objective, what it must be feeling out there in that unending solitude. Only by pretending that inanimate objects were somehow alive could man feel any link with the machines he sent off into distant space. It was like someone trying to move numb and frozen toes to make sure they were still part of his body. To reassure ourselves that this probe flying beyond the asteroid belt was still part of our world, we tried to envisage ourselves flying out there along with it. It became a seeing eye whose field of vision we imagined we shared, just as we imagined the endless desolation of a place where there was literally nothing. Many people must have fallen under the spell of that illusion.

Canna's existence in relation to his was now, perhaps, not unlike the unmanned space probe's. She was flying in a different world. Now and again she sent reports about sights he hadn't seen for himself, but the distance between them continued to grow, the electromagnetic waves took longer to arrive— hours now—until eventually he would no longer know what amazing landscapes she was looking at on some far-off planet. She wouldn't belong to her father's world any more but to the world of the stars. He wondered if she would feel lonely there, but perhaps there would be enough to interest her in the way of strange phenomena to keep her occupied ... And then he told himself to stop, feeling he'd got lost in a long, winding maze of sentimental thoughts. As he sank into sleep his only remaining thought was that the universe was wide, too wide in fact, as was the world we human beings ourselves lived in.

"Don't you have a wife, Mr. Takatsu?" Khukin asked.

They were eating together for the second time, although this time Canna wasn't with them.

"We separated. Around four years ago."

"I see. Please forgive my intrusion."

"I don't mind particularly. It's not so unusual these days, though perhaps it's not too common for the father to be raising the child."

"Quite so. But, of course, you have a very bright daughter."

"Given her age, I hardly feel I'm raising her, actually. It's all so different from when we had to worry about baby food and nurseries. In fact it's probably truer to say she's raising herself and I'm just watching from the sidelines. Maybe I lend a hand occasionally."

"I see."

"Do you yourself have any family?" Fumihiko said in return.

"I do, but they are in Irkutsk. A wife and three children. The elder two are boys and the youngest a girl. I got married rather early, so the elder two have already graduated from university. I have not seen them all for a long time, ever since I came to work in Japan alone in fact. I am trying to arrange things so that I can go back soon."

"You said you'd spent ten years here."

"Yes, indeed—a very, very long ten years. Fortunately it was not the ten years when children have most need of the presence of a father. They are all quite big now, I suppose. I have tried to make up by writing frequent letters." Khukin gazed into the distance for a while, then turned back to Fumihiko. "I imagine it must be quite a job living alone with your daughter."

"Yes. I have to do rather more than my normal share of the housework. But we have a maid come in once a week and Canna certainly does her bit. At least she does much more than a child in a household where there's a mother to do the work.

She's never been a dependent child, or particularly close to her parents. Of course, her parents weren't all that close either."

Khukin nodded.

"Her mother was always the type who preferred to be out in the big, wide world. I myself am not exactly an office worker, but I still have an office I have to go to. So right from the start Canna lived in a different world from her parents, getting together with friends or wrapped up in something she was doing on her own. If she was with her friends, they'd be playing at acrobats; if she was on her own, she'd be practicing handstands or something. Even now, she doesn't show any signs of missing her mother. She doesn't seem to think it's that important for her parents to live together."

But was that true? He had never asked her directly. A marriage had broken up. A child had lost her mother or at least become independent of her mother at a very early age. As a high school student, she was leading a slightly abnormal life. No doubt she would quickly grow independent of her father. He could see her living quite happily on her own, getting a good job, then coming to visit him occasionally out of a sense of duty. Quite possibly she would end up going abroad.

One could only guess what might have happened if a different road had been taken. There was no way of telling how she might have grown up if her mother had stayed, just as there had been no way of comparing the two roads at the time and choosing the better one. Did Canna feel envious of children living in normal households and, if she did, how deeply? He had no way of knowing.

When they'd finished dinner they went to a bar, where they drank fairly late into the night, though afterward he didn't remember actually feeling drunk. They talked a lot. Khukin insisted that he call him Pavel, and then gave a very lengthy account of his life, of growing up in Irkutsk, going to Moscow, returning to Irkutsk, spending a long time in Leningrad and, finally, coming to Japan. As the liquor loosened his tongue, Khukin's Japanese began to sound more and more Russian: his carefully filed down Japanese consonants took on the heavy bronze resonance of Russian, even though his grammar and vocabulary remained unchanged.

But he certainly knew how to tell a good story. Fumihiko often found himself laughing as he listened to his rich supply of childhood reminiscences. Fumihiko then talked about himself, wondering why he was telling this man so much and listening to so much in exchange. What a strange encounter it was that had produced this friendship. He listened to him talk about Siberia. Maybe the "wide world" was only as wide as this. Maybe it was a small world, really; a small world, and what mattered was the people in it. Yes, it's people that matter, he concluded, finally realizing at that point that he was well and truly drunk.

The third time they met was at an indoor skating rink. This had been Khukin's idea, as was the suggestion that Canna come as well. Fumihiko hadn't skated for twenty years, but his body soon remembered how to do it. Canna, on the other hand, had only roller-skated when she was small, and this was her first time on ice skates. For three turns around the rink she clung to her father's hand, but once she'd learned how to balance on the blades she soon got the hang of it. She didn't fall over once.

"No need to worry about getting lost in the fog here, anyway," she whispered in his ear, and when he turned to look at her she had flashed away to the other side of the rink, weaving nimbly between the other beginners, who were stumbling around and lurching forward like apes. He was impressed.

What was truly impressive, though, was the way Khukin per-

formed. He was wearing his everyday dark suit, but after slipping on the skates he'd brought with him and stepping lightly
onto the ice, he was a man transformed. Fumihiko watched as
the slight clumsiness that usually marked his gait vanished and
he sped away with an expert flourish of his blades. Keeping his
body low, he made several circuits of the rink in almost no time
at all. One could see the difference that growing up in Siberia
must have made: he was obviously far more accomplished at it
than Fumihiko was. But there was more to come. After he had
been around a few more times, he skated smartly over to where
Fumihiko was standing, removed his jacket and tossed it to him.

"If you wouldn't mind holding this a moment," he said casually, and took off in shirtsleeves and tie for the middle of the
rink, where he proceeded to give an impromptu demonstration
of figure skating. Some people were already doing figures there,
but even to an amateur's eye their skills were minimal. Once
Khukin got going they all stopped and watched. He was clearly
back in his element. He performed a variety of moves, shifting
his weight effortlessly from one leg to the other and switching
the angle of his blades, all in a single, smooth, uninterrupted
rhythm. When he cut a figure eight its symmetry was impeccable.

A crowd formed about him, and since Canna was skating
fairly well now Fumihiko left her and went to join them, standing slightly back with his arms folded, watching Khukin practice
his skills. When Khukin performed a double spin jump, a young
man beside Fumihiko gave an audible gasp at his faultless landing.

"He's terrific," said another voice at his side. It was Canna,
who had slipped her hand into his and was watching Khukin
admiringly.

"Yes. Terrific."

"Usually he looks like some middle-aged bumpkin just up from the country, but he's completely different here."

"That's how he seemed to you?"

"What else did you expect? Just look at the shape he's in and the way he smiles all the time. All middle-aged spread and as clumsy as they come. But he's really something on skates, I have to admit."

"Since he's this good it's no wonder he invites people to go skating."

Khukin went on skating for twenty minutes or so, then suddenly stopped, looked in Canna's direction and, with a smile, came over.

"You're really good," said Canna in a voice that showed genuine respect.

"I am a bit out of practice, I'm afraid," he replied modestly.

"Have you ever entered any competitions?"

"Just once, when I was sixteen, in Khabarovsk. I was all right by myself, but quite hopeless at pair skating, so I came nowhere near the medals. After that I just kept my hand in, as it were, doing a little instructing at the club. Since coming to Japan I have been here occasionally, but I am not obsessive about it."

"I wish I could learn."

"Then I will teach you. You are a gymnast, so you will soon become proficient at it."

"Dad, is it all right if I learn how to skate?" she asked.

"If you're quite sure you really want to."

"Of course I am, especially when I'm lucky enough to have such a great teacher," she replied without hesitating.

It seemed her father could hardly refuse. Canna had always made up her mind quickly and it was best simply to let her have her own way.

In a whispered conversation on the ice, Khukin and Canna

had soon worked out an arrangement for her to have lessons twice a month, every other Sunday.

At home that evening Canna spoke in an unusually subdued voice about her limitations as a gymnast.

"I don't think I'm actually going to get any better at it. I've peaked. Physically I've grown too big, and all the top gymnasts are in their early teens nowadays anyway. It gets more and more acrobatic all the time, and the average age keeps going down."

"That's been the tendency for the past ten years. What Chaslavska did at twenty-two Comaneci did at fourteen."

"But Comaneci did much harder things. They called her 'the machine,' and that was ten years ago. I know I've improved over the last two years, but it all felt much easier two years ago and I'm not moving as well any more. I feel I'm just forcing myself, without getting any better, so this year's championships will probably be my last."

"So you won't do gymnastics at university?"

"No. I'll go to an ordinary university. I never thought I wanted to make a career of gymnastics, anyway. That's why I never joined a club but just did it at school. Coaching some of the younger ones will be enough for me. Instead I'll be enjoying myself skating, hah, hah."

So she'd be taking her college entrance exams next year. Well, maybe that was best. She read a lot, and whenever she asked him about problems in math or physics that she couldn't quite work out she was never far off the mark. She still had plenty of time to find out what she wanted to do. At least, he told himself, it didn't look as if she'd be going to Russia for further training.

Eventually it became an established routine for him to spend one or two evenings a month drinking with Khukin, while

Canna took skating lessons from him every second and fourth Sunday. Khukin seemed to enjoy both.

"Don't you ever feel you want to go back to Russia?" Fumihiko once asked him.

"Yes, I do. I want to revisit certain places. I want to ride a horse over the snow. I also want to see my wife, and there are many things I would like to eat. Sometimes the feeling is almost unbearable. I picture to myself the streets of Irkutsk in great detail, wandering around them in my head."

"Yes, I can imagine," said Fumihiko, feeling a bit sorry for him.

"I am trying to arrange my return as soon as possible. But my work in lumber exporting has been highly successful, and besides, my superiors seem to hold to the policy that it would be unwise to let someone as good at Japanese as I am live permanently in Russia. So they don't want to let me go home."

"Well, your Japanese *is* very good."

"For some days now I have been thinking about the difference between a feeling for the place one was born in and the concept of patriotism."

"Why?"

"If you live abroad, you would think that the two would be one and the same thing, yet in my case it has been somewhat different. When I first came to Japan, all I felt was patriotism, but now, after so many years, the hold of the Soviet Union on my mind has diminished, while the gravitational pull of my home town has grown infinitely stronger. Patriotism has vanished and only my love for my home remains. Being a good Soviet citizen does not matter to me any more. I have become a sentimental Siberian. So it is time for me to go home."

"I see."

"I no longer have sufficient patriotism to motivate me. So if, for example, I felt that you, Mr. Takatsu, might be the kind of person who was prepared to supply certain information to our country, I would not know how to broach the matter to you."

"I'm sorry, I don't quite follow."

"I was able to tell from your business card precisely what kind of work you are involved in. As far as we, meaning the Soviet Union, are concerned, this work is bound to be of some interest to us."

"Yes, I can see that."

"Therefore, if I were able to persuade you to tell us what you know about the communication systems used by the Japanese Self-Defense Forces, I would be making a considerable contribution to my country. That is what I have been thinking about these past few days, that I should persuade you to do so by means of my own special theory of the nature of world peace. If I were the same man I was nine years ago I would be putting this plan into action immediately. However, being the way I am now and having reflected on it carefully, I find I would be unable to proceed with any real enthusiasm."

"It's just as well. After all, if you were anything like what you suggest you were nine years ago, we wouldn't be drinking together like this."

"You are no doubt right."

"I suppose there always was the possibility that Pavel Ivanovich Khukin worked for the KGB, and that's why he approached me in the first place."

"That, however, is not the case. I am an absolutely bona fide businessman who has been involved with nothing but lumber every day for the past ten years."

"But how would a bona fide businessman be able to persuade me to become a spy?"

"In a perfectly amateurish way, like a back-seat driver or ...

how do you say it here?—a barstool lawyer. Would you like to hear? You have to understand, I have been thinking in this way for a long time now. Perhaps what I have to say is no more than a reflection of the way the Russian intelligentsia has always thought about such questions—things such as the existence of the state and the world situation, about peace and about our country's backwardness."

"I'd very much like to hear."

"Where we want to end up is knowing if you, Mr. Takatsu, would give information to us, but it will take time to reach that point. First we must deal with world history since the end of the Second World War.

"I myself was born during that dreadful war and grew up in the miserable years that followed, as, I believe, you also did. Since then we have been continually on the brink of another war. The two great powers possess huge arsenals of missiles as well as myriad tanks and submarines. There have been several minor wars. And yet I believe these past forty years have been essentially peaceful ones. There has been no major war. And why not? Because of what is usually referred to as the balance of power."

"The idea that an equal balance of atomic weapons acts as a deterrent is an illusion the military types on both sides share," Fumihiko demurred.

"I agree. But it has worked. Let the military types keep their illusion. You know, this world is not really divided into East and West, but into the illusory world of the military and the actual world of ordinary people. You could describe it as an illusory purgatory and a potentially real hell. If the balance of power can be maintained between the two power blocs that represent purgatory, then they will have no impact on the real world. In this way, all the rumblings of war can be strictly confined to their fantasy world. The important thing is to be able to distinguish between the world of illusion and the world of reality and then keep this East–West balance going in the illusory one."

"All right. But what has this got to do with my work?"

"Let's not cross our bridges before we come to them," said Khukin with a slight smile. "What matters is the fact that a balance of power should be maintained, not the means by which it is maintained. If that aim is achieved, by whatever method, and always assuming some dreadful accident does not occur, then peace can be preserved."

"The end justifies the means, meaning that the development of new weapons may be evil but stealing the secrets of the enemy's weapons is good."

"That is correct. There are three ways of achieving this balance of power. The first is by addition: you add to those areas where you have less than your enemy. The arms race, in fact. The second is by subtraction: you subtract from those areas where you have too much. This is disarmament or arms reduction, which, in fact, is extremely difficult to do. There is a third method, however, which we may refer to as the mirror strategy. This means that you create an exact replica of what your enemy possesses. Since you cannot actually steal your enemy's tanks you create a tank with an identical capability. And how do you do this? You borrow his plans. Political pressure may be needed to achieve such a balance in terms of quantity, but, as far as quality is concerned, all that is required is information."

"So my role would be to supplement those areas in which you're short of information?"

"No, nothing quite as simple as that. Think of it in this way. In response to the military's illusory world, the information agencies create a mirror world that makes a paradise of their purgatory. It is like a foreign currency market where false notes of credit called military information are exchanged, and these illusory notes perform the role of maintaining the balance that the market requires. In order to ensure that either party in the exchange does not become too powerful, we create a circuit that permits what could be called a feedback."

"An interesting argument, but it's all pure theory, of course."

"No. I disagree. Each state inevitably produces a military capability suited to its size. The key thing is neither the quantity nor the quality of their weapons, but that the weapons should be in equilibrium with other countries. The one real, the one truly powerful effect of atomic weapons is that they have forced us to recognize that reality."

"It's dangerous, all this."

"You mean atomic weapons? Well, everybody agrees they are."

"No. I mean it's dangerous to speculate about what's behind the business of acquiring this kind of information. People steal information from each other for immediate profit, something they can see right in front of their noses. They're not interested in artificial notes of credit to stabilize the market. They're looking for results. Plain old nationalism is the most powerful motive —the idea of actually upsetting the balance of power and seeing your own country on top."

"That is why it is so important to have real professionals involved in the information game; not people who are overflowing with loyalty to their country, but those who feel a strong involvement with the information suppliers in the opposite camp. I, a Siberian lumber merchant, am propounding to you a new theory of information exchange, an ideal, if you like. My argument goes like this. Technology produces new weapons. New weapons are dangerous. The danger can be neutralized by an exchange of information concerning the new weapons."

"In these dealings, can we be confident the exchange rate will be maintained?" asked Fumihiko, rather taken aback by Khukin's penchant for abstract argument and feeling he'd somehow been put on the defensive.

"I don't know. In any given instance, one side will go into the red, no doubt, but this does not matter since the accounts will balance out in the long term. Or think of it in this way. A ship strikes a reef and tears a hole in its side. Water pours in. Since it is coming in on only one side there is a danger the ship may capsize before it sinks. When the angle becomes too steep you can no longer use the water pumps. Even if pumps are theoretically useful when your ship is sinking, in this particular case the principle no longer applies. So what do you do?"

"Flood both sides equally to achieve balance."

"Exactly. When the problem is not the amount of water coming in but the difference in level between the port and starboard sides, you have to make up your mind to violate the most basic principle of seamanship and let water in on the side without the hole as well. After that you can use the pumps to get rid of the excess water, and the ship will not sink."

"Well, that all makes a kind of general, abstract sense, and within its limits I'm prepared to admit the argument is interesting—I might even say it was valid, to a certain extent. But the real question is still to come, and it concerns me, myself. Everything you've said so far might seem relevant to someone up in the stands just watching the game, but what about the person out there on the mound pitching? What reason is there for me, me, to risk my skin in order to test your theory? Why should I break the Japanese law and completely ignore my own conscience as well? There can't be a reason good enough."

"That, of course, is the problem. My reasons have all been persuasive so far, but I lack the power to coax you over this final hurdle. I could produce several arguments, but in reality there is not much besides idealism that will induce a person to become a supplier of information."

"What about financial rewards?"

"Well, my country could hardly afford to pay you in foreign currencies. And I imagine you would not be happy with rubles. If you were prepared to spend your retirement in Irkutsk, however, no doubt adequate arrangements could be made."

"One of those weekend cottages, what are they called …?"

"Yes, a dacha on Lake Baikal has its attractions."

"I think I'd prefer something on one of our islands in the Northern Territories."

"Now we are pushing a bit too hard," said Khukin, raising his glass to his lips. "Which all goes to show," he went on, "how unrealistic such demands are. A good agent does not work for financial rewards but for philosophical reasons. That just brings me back to what I was saying before, I admit, but I must insist again that I have given the subject a great deal of thought. What kind of efforts are needed on our part to maintain the sandhill of peace at its present height? How, in fact, can information be exchanged?"

"And the next metaphor will be your sinking ship again, twisted logic and all."

"Twisted? I thought it made very good sense myself."

"It makes sense in its context, but only in its context. And it wouldn't even make sense there if you saw me as an actual passenger on that ship. I'm aware that the ship may be sinking, but I only consider myself a passenger, not a member of the crew."

"So in fact I have failed to persuade you?"

"It struck me a little while ago that ever since the war ended you, you Russians, have been obsessed with America, seeing yourselves as a mirror image of it. As a result you've been continually overreaching yourselves."

"You call it overreaching?"

"I do. Both economically and technologically, you've had only half their resources in real terms, and yet you've gone on knocking yourselves out trying to achieve parity. That's why you've been so backward in producing consumer goods, why you've been so repressive at home and why you've attracted so much criticism from outside. And one target of that criticism has been the activities of what you call your information agencies."

"Which is precisely the situation I have been trying to explain in various ways. It all returns to the fact that, as I have said, a balance must be maintained. Call it vanity in our case, but it is the vanity of a paper bear. The only way peace can be preserved is by accepting a scenario in which the two great powers remain in competition with each other. The Americans made atomic weapons, so we imitated them and made our own, even if we did wonder why these things were necessary in the first place. If it is a mirror, then it is one in which the Americans have done everything first and we have been running like mad just to keep up."

"Do you think you ought to be saying things like that?"

"Ten years ago I wouldn't have, but I have been observing the world since I came to Japan, and thinking about things. I started wondering why our great, cold, northern country should be so poor, why there was never enough food to go around. This is just between you and me, but I came to the following conclusion. In order to maintain peace, what we needed above anything else was military security. If America was stronger than us, obviously stronger, then we would be under pressure in every aspect of our existence. Even defending our own soil would be a problem. If the pressure grew too great, the possibility of taking desperate retaliation would become very real. And in the atomic age, retaliation is dangerous, highly dangerous. So we clung fast to the idea of equilibrium—an illusion, if you like, but we clung to it anyway. The balance of power came first, no matter how wicked our reputation might become, no matter how much we might have to reduce our children's rations of milk. It was our obsession, our persecution complex, perhaps. But for forty years there has been no major war."

"Okay. That's certainly one way of looking at it, though I'd rather like to hear the reactions to your point of view in the streets of Warsaw or Prague or Kabul."

"No doubt the people there would have different points of view."

"I can understand what you're saying—about the basic innocence of Russian intentions and therefore of your intelligence agencies—but in concrete terms I'm not persuaded. The only thing that means anything to me here and now is the presence of one man, Pavel Ivanovich Khukin. His country means nothing to me. So, as far as persuading me to give you information goes, you don't have any good cards to play. Let's leave it at that for today. We can continue the argument some other time, but it's about time we went home. Under the circumstances I think we should split the bill."

"Yes, indeed. I never imagined I would be able to buy your services with whiskey and vodka. Still, today is just today. I believe you ought to think it over a little."

With that, Khukin's expression returned to normal and a smile spread over his face.

3

I said earlier that I'd probably still be looking after Diplodocus when I was an old lady, and that if I couldn't afford it I might even consider doing something criminal. But the truth is I probably won't be able to keep Dippy for very long. I think the day will come when I'll no longer be up to it.

Just a few days ago Dippy didn't eat the feed I got ready for him. I had other things to do and had to leave the house early. I felt bad about it, but I took down the balcony railing at eleven o'clock, got his special hay ready and then left. It had happened before, and Dippy had always come right on time and eaten his feed on his own even if I wasn't around. But when I came back that day I saw that he hadn't touched a thing.

What made it worse was that it had rained heavily and the hay was all wet. Diplodocus eats the grass in the meadow even when it's raining, but he won't touch the special hay if it's wet. On rainy days I always keep an eye on him while he's eating, feeding him one bundle of hay at a time (though, come to think of it, it didn't rain that day till late afternoon, so that couldn't have been the reason Dippy didn't eat). Anyway, I just put all the wet hay in the bathroom for the time being.

The next day I got some new hay ready on the balcony just before twelve o'clock, feeling pretty nervous as I waited for him. Dippy came right on time. He didn't seem at all annoyed about my not being there the day before and ate his hay up happily as usual.

"I'm really sorry about yesterday, Dippy. I had to go somewhere," I told him. "Next time I leave your hay for you, you will eat it up, won't you?" But he just went on chewing quietly, and I don't know if he heard me or not.

Still, as I was feeding the bundles of hay one by one into his huge mouth I started thinking. What probably upset him, I decided, wasn't my not being there at twelve o'clock but the fact that I've started to find other interests, that I'm beginning to look out into the big, wide world. If the world consisted only of me and Dippy and the meadow, then I'd still be looking after him when I was an old lady. Everything would work out fine and I wouldn't even have to do anything bad when I got old. In fact I wouldn't grow old, I'd always be just the same as I am now. The special hay would arrive from China every week without fail, and every afternoon on the appointed day I would wait for the 140 bundles of hay to be dropped by parachute from the plane. But the truth is I can't go on playing with Diplodocus forever.

Anyway, after Dippy had gone off quite cheerfully to the far side of the meadow, I hauled the bundles of damp hay out of the bathroom and up onto the roof to try to dry them. It was a very windy day, so I couldn't untie the bundles in case they blew away. I tried to dry them as they were, all tied up, but they wouldn't dry right through to the middle. By the next day they all smelled really nasty. I was terribly disappointed because it meant I couldn't feed them to Dippy as they might make him sick. In the end I took all twenty bundles of the stuff to an open area and burned them. The smoke rose high into the sky.

The next morning I decided to go and play in the meadow. I almost never meet Dippy anywhere except on our balcony, but I was feeling lonely, so after washing the breakfast dishes, I put on my boots and set off toward the woods out there in the distance. I thought I might come across Dippy somewhere.

But no matter which path I took, I couldn't see his great big shape anywhere. I told myself he was probably still asleep but, even if he was, I ought to be able to see something that big, so I went on walking right through the woods and into another meadow, and Dippy wasn't there either. It occurred to me that he might have headed north or south. My Diplodocus usually just goes back and forth between the hills to the west and my place in the east, and doesn't venture very far north or south. Also Dippy doesn't walk too far when he's just got up. I started to feel a bit worried. Maybe he'd actually set off for some faraway place yesterday and had been walking since yesterday afternoon. If he didn't plan on coming back, maybe I'd never find him.

I walked right to the far end of the meadow and still couldn't see him, but just as I was on the verge of giving up and going home, I turned around and saw a black, round shape at the southern edge of the wood. It looked very like the curved back of a diplodocus. I ran toward it, my boots making a funny squelching sound as I splashed through puddles. The closer I got the more plainly I could see that it was the back of my Dippy.

Now that I was close, Dippy lifted his head slowly and looked in my direction. I stood in front of him and raised both hands— my usual morning greeting. Dippy stretched out his long neck and brought his face close to mine. It was the same lovable old face I saw every day at the edge of the balcony. I took a step forward and pummeled him. Dippy looked really happy and nuzzled me gently, very gently, with his nose. I hugged his head with both my arms. As always, he smelled of so many things: his hay-scented breath, the dew on the meadow, even a very faint smell of dung.

I walked all around him, punching his folded legs and his long curving tail and his plump belly and saying, "Oh, Dippy!" over and over. Dippy closed his eyes and kept absolutely still, making sure he didn't accidentally squash me.

I realized it was already past eleven o'clock. Since it had been my idea to come out here, it would be my fault if I was late with his hay. I told Dippy I was going back to the balcony to get his feed ready and he was to come on time for it, then hurried home. I ran so hard I was completely out of breath when I got there. By the time Dippy's head could be seen swaying toward us in the dis-

tance, I had twenty bundles of hay lined up on the balcony, and I
watched with a funny mixture of feelings as he approached.

Khukin did not get in touch with Fumihiko again for two or
three weeks, although Canna still went to the ice rink on her
scheduled days for skating lessons. She told Fumihiko proudly
about her smooth backward figure eight.

He had thought the discussion of the other evening would
soon be forgotten, but found instead that it continued to distract him. The proposal that had been made was, of course,
ridiculous, but he caught himself imagining how it would feel if
he did go along with it and started providing Khukin with information. First he would tell him everything he already knew,
then he would set about acquiring as much new information as
he could and passing it over at fixed intervals. He would, in
effect, become a spy. The odd thing was that he found the
prospect definitely attractive. Its appeal, however, had nothing
to do with the simple notions Khukin had tried to put across or
with whatever financial rewards he might receive, or even with
the vague fondness he felt for Russia. No, what attracted him
was the act itself, the idea of passing information to someone
on the other side of the border.

The bottom line about spying was that it called for a dual
personality. Just living a normal, everyday life required a full
immersion in the world, a constant semi-awareness of its customs and values, of what the world considered common sense,
trying hard each day to stay within those confines. But becoming a spy meant simultaneously and secretly belonging to
another system, one with values utterly opposed to those of the
everyday world. You spent each day as two different people. It
was no longer a question of straying from the norm by a hairs-
breadth or so, but a deliberate denial of the social code at its

deepest level, a silent rejection of the imposture by which different countries are permitted different codes in the first place.

When that kind of person engages in ordinary conversation, inwardly he is constantly sizing up, calculating, seeing the world from a completely different perspective to that of other people. No matter whom he talks to, something inside him is silently saying: You may think this is a real person you see before you, but in fact that person is completely hidden. Someone who belongs to two ethical systems truly belongs to neither of them, and is thus free of both.

In a case like this, talk of selling information or selling out one's country or amassing huge sums in a secret Swiss bank account is deceptive: what really matters is the act of freeing oneself from the restraints of two ethical systems by exploiting the gaps between them. Fumihiko knew he would get a kick out of handling a miniature camera, using the Xerox alone late at night in the office, hiding radio and scrambler in a cupboard at home, and casually feeding questions to people with access to official secrets, even though he knew that any sense of achievement these things could provide was ultimately meaningless. Spies didn't act for the sake of ideals (which was why Khukin's political arguments had been unconvincing), or for money, or for the prospect of an easy life when they retired, but simply to enjoy a freedom of action that would probably be considered illegal in either of the countries involved. Even his handlers would secretly despise him in their hearts, looking on him as a crook who was in it only for the money. They were just using him, they'd claim. Yet none of this would matter to him; it was for that heady taste of freedom that he would be prepared to continue, year after year after year, in a life spent constantly looking over his shoulder.

And that wasn't all. He would be free of other people's judgments. It would no longer matter what anybody said, because whatever he did—failing or achieving, seducing female colleagues or trying unsuccessfully to give up smoking, arranging flowers every day on his desk or staying rooted in some chronic habit—all this would concern a purely temporary self. His real self would be in a no-man's-land between two countries, with information at his fingertips that would cost billions, maybe even trillions, if sought by regular, direct methods. Neither praise nor blame could penetrate as thick a skin as his. He would be untouchable.

Could he endure the constant threat of prison or execution for the sake of such a freedom? In practice, of course, his true worth as a person would any properly be known when he'd been finally exposed and put on trial. On that day everyone around him—his colleagues, neighborhood shopkeepers, old school acquaintances, distant relatives—would understand the true meaning, the sheer scale of what he'd secretly done, and they would be amazed. And when he climbed up to the scaffold it would be as if he were ascending a royal throne; he would be a lion released from a morality made for mice.

But Fumihiko's fantasy remained just that—a fantasy. A real spy, who genuinely believed in what he was doing and was willing to accept the sacrifices his double life entailed, would still, to all intents and purposes, be leading a very ordinary, sober existence. All he would have to look forward to would be medals he could never display and a dishonored name to bequeath to history. Fumihiko wondered if such people really existed. Certainly it was a way of life he personally would find impossible. To take even the first step toward it would call for a kind of heroism, albeit of a perverse kind; and for a man like himself with few complaints about his daily life it was utterly out of the question.

On the evening of the very day he'd been thinking these things, his Russian friend phoned, with an almost telepathic sense of timing. Khukin sounded quite cheerful, just as he had before the subject had been broached.

"How are you getting on, Mr. Takatsu? Very well, I trust."

"Yes, fine. And you?"

"All right, I suppose. But I am a greedy person, you know, and I always hope to feel even better. I was wondering if you would like to join me for a blowfish dinner?"

"Blowfish?"

"Why not? It is the most delicious fish—there is nothing quite like it. And I know a very good restaurant. Won't you join me?"

"Well, all right."

"Good. How about tomorrow evening?"

"Fine. I've nothing planned for tomorrow and, anyway, you've now given me this craving to eat blowfish ..."

He found the idea decidedly eccentric, but fixed a time and place for the following day and hung up. Although he had answered civilly enough, the prospect actually depressed him. He felt he simply didn't have the energy to go on arguing with Khukin about the same things. What worried him was that, if Khukin ever got off the subject of Russia and its aims and began discussing Fumihiko's work, there was a question he felt he had no adequate answer to. Why was he involved in the development of technology for military rather than civilian purposes? He was sure that even a casual conversation would eventually end up at this awkward question, revealing his own feelings of guilt about what he was doing. This was the real weakness at the core of any counterargument he might make, and he knew it. The debate would be tough. He liked blowfish and he imagined that eating it might give him extra zest. But then, Khukin would be eating it too.

He realized he'd better go out and do some shopping; there was still time before Canna was due back from her gym practice. He got into the car and drove to the supermarket, where he stocked up on groceries. As he was carrying the bags to the car, he found himself thinking again how convenient it would be if you could bring the shopping carts out to the parking lot. Canna's face came to mind and he smiled wryly.

When Canna got home at eight she noticed the fridge was full again.

"Oh no! You're not going away again?"

"No. Nothing like that. I just felt like doing a bit of shopping."

"And you bought all this? You're hopeless."

"We'll manage."

"You can manage by yourself. Leave me out of it."

When Canna had finished eating she went straight to her room. He could hear her voice on the phone for a long time, apparently speaking not just to one but several people. The unmanned space probe was sending messages to different stars. The distance between the space probe and the earth was growing gradually but unmistakably greater all the time.

The next day, Fumihiko put in his hours at work doing various chores and attending pointless meetings, then left early to keep his appointment. Khukin was in a remarkably good mood, behaving as if their dramatic discussion had never taken place; it made Fumihiko wonder how he looked himself. The place Khukin took him to was a traditional Japanese restaurant of some distinction. Judging from the friendly, almost familiar greeting of the proprietress, who looked as if she might have been a geisha in her younger days and was courteous to a fault, the Russian was a valued customer there.

"You know some pretty exotic places."

"I invite my customers here. Since it is a very capitalistic practice, I have considerable difficulty getting my superiors to accept it. Luckily I am allowed to balance my own books, for the most part. Another, off-the-record reason for coming here is that the restaurant gives me quite a large discount. So I return the courtesy by trying to avoid those times of the year when the place is busy."

"That's a very Japanese way to behave."

"Well, when you have lived somewhere for ten years ..."

Fumihiko hadn't eaten blowfish for some time and it tasted delicious. Khukin handled his chopsticks with skill, neatly conveying three of the thin slices of raw fish to his mouth each time. His long acquaintance with the country was obvious: he was perfectly at ease, knew the correct way to eat blowfish and actually appreciated its exotic taste. And yet his homesickness persisted. That was just the way things were.

Fumihiko introduced the term "des-pot" into the conversation, explaining that it referred to someone who, at one of those meals where everyone shared a common pot, was always telling other people what to do, saying this bit was nicely cooked or that bit wasn't ready yet or warning them not to eat all the meat. He said he was often scolded by Canna for behaving that way at home. The waitress who was serving them overheard this and laughed, prompting Khukin to wonder aloud what the Russian equivalent would be; he came up with several phrases, but shook his head at all of them.

They both concentrated on eating rather than drinking; in fact they set about it so earnestly for a while there was no chance to talk about anything serious. Fumihiko mentioned the way Canna got annoyed with him for buying too much food, which made Khukin roar with laughter. When he had recovered, however, Fumihiko said suddenly:

"About what we were saying the other day—I'm afraid it's no go."

The meal was almost over. All that remained on the table were the nearly empty earthenware pot, the odd dish and the plates of fruit they hadn't yet touched. Their waitress had disappeared.

"Ah, you mean that business about spying," Khukin said. He spoke quite casually. "Well, I never thought there was much chance in your case. From the very start I was merely enjoying a friendly discussion. But since you did not come up with any very strong arguments against the idea, I wanted you to think about it a little more deeply."

Fumihiko felt suddenly deflated. "You mean I've been worrying myself to death about nothing?"

"In the event that you had taken the suggestion seriously, I would probably have been more inclined to talk you out of it. In fact I had not even thought about what to do next if you had said yes."

"After handing me over to one of your experts you could have applied for the Order of Lenin."

"Good idea, the Order of Lenin. Still, that is all over with now. I apologize for ever having introduced such a foolish topic. And as an expression of my contrition I shall treat you this evening as my own private guest."

"No, I can't accept that. This place is much too expensive. We'll split the bill. Sometime in the future you can treat me to some shashlik in a restaurant in Irkutsk."

"That is a Caucasus dish. We do not have it in Siberia. But there are many good things to eat in Irkutsk."

"Then I'll order everything in advance; way in advance, in fact, since it'll probably be years before I go there."

"No one knows what fate has in store for him," he replied in a strangely quiet voice.

"A solemn thought," said Fumihiko. "An overly solemn thought in this case. Incidentally, I don't think I'll go on somewhere else this evening, I want to go straight home if that's all right with you."

"It suits me very well. There is still some business I have to do."

On his way home in the taxi Fumihiko thought that he would tell Canna about this some day, but since it touched directly on his work, he couldn't do it for a while. He imagined a time, though, when he'd have a completely different job and the three of them would be sitting around a table laughing about it all. But when, he wondered, would that be?

Three days later he had to stay late at the office, though not so late it could be called overtime. Arriving home a little past his usual time, he saw from outside that Canna had apparently got back before him, as every light in the place was on.

He went up to the fifth floor in the elevator, and when he opened the front door was astonished by the number of shoes in the entrance hall. Cheerful voices could be heard farther inside. What on earth was she up to, he wondered, finally managing to find a place for his own shoes.

Their living room was not particularly small, but the ten or so young people in it filled it to overflowing. As he peered tentatively in, someone noticed him, setting off a chorus of conventional greetings: "Welcome back!" "Sorry for being here!" He merely raised his hand in reply, looking around for Canna.

"Oh hello, Daddy, are you back?" she said, emerging from the kitchen just then with a large platter of food.

"What's going on? Having a party?"

"Well, you did buy all that food, so I thought I'd try to get rid of some of it by asking this lot around."

"Did I buy enough for ten?" he said, glancing around the room.

"I did have to get a bit more, actually. And they brought some with them. We did the cooking ourselves. Some of them are pretty good at it. Not as good as me, of course."

"Come off it. Tomoyuki's going to be a real chef."

"Well, you can shut up, for a start. It just so happens that *I* have a natural gift for it."

This statement was greeted with mingled assents and jeers, restoring the atmosphere to the way it had been just before he turned up.

"Anyway, Dad, have something to eat," said Canna.

Fumihiko was obliged to sit down in this noisy crowd, choosing a corner seat and rather wishing they could have found somewhere else for their party. The girl next to him promptly passed him a small plate and chopsticks. He'd seen her a few times before, but couldn't remember her name. Canna was often annoyed by his inability to remember her friends' names.

"My God, they've got beer," he said.

"Yes, but only one can each," he heard his daughter's distant voice protesting.

The food was surprisingly good considering that they'd all prepared it together—better, certainly, than the kind of meal the average housewife produced. He looked over at Canna, who was now doling out some freshly cooked fish with a pair of long chopsticks, and wondered if she often did this sort of thing when he was away from home. She looked like someone else, a young woman he'd never seen before.

The party consisted of four other girls and five boys. Some of them were fellow gymnasts at school, some were in Canna's class or were friends from middle school who had kept in touch. The fact that Canna's father had somehow joined one of their get-togethers seemed not to have dampened their high spirits. They were all extremely talkative, but when he spoke to them individually, he found they were polite and articulate, not just a bunch of youngsters having a good time.

Still, it was only natural that he should feel uncomfortable there, so he decided to retire to another room, and quickly polished off his food. Just as he was about to move, though, the phone rang. He signaled to Canna that he would answer it, went into his room, turned on the light and picked up the receiver.

"Hello. Is that Mr. Takatsu?"

"Oh, it's you. Thanks again for the meal the other night," he told the caller, Khukin.

"We did share the bill, remember? Anyway, I have something to tell you. Do you recall how, just before we left that night, I said that no one ever knows what fate has in store for him and you laughed at me for being overly solemn?"

"I didn't actually laugh at you."

"Well, the fact is that fate has ordained a change in my life."

"Really?"

"I shall be returning home."

"Oh, congratulations—if, of course, congratulations are in order. I take it that this isn't an ignominious demotion but a triumphant return?"

"I wish you would not use such difficult words, but, yes, it is all right, I can go with my head held high. I have been trying to arrange it for a long time now. As I have told you on numerous occasions, I have been here for a good ten years."

"Where are you being transferred to?"

"I am not, in fact, being transferred. I am changing my profession. I shall be going to Irkutsk. You remember, the first time we met, I talked about a Japanese language school, the very first one established abroad? I am going to become a teacher at that school. And I intend to do some translation work as well."

"Then I really can congratulate you. That's great news. You will be an excellent teacher."

"It is my hope, therefore, that you really will come and visit us. Miss Canna as well. We can skate, we can drink vodka, we can eat all kinds of delicious food. You did say you wanted to see Siberia?"

"Yes, very much so. But unfortunately I can't travel by air."

"Of course, you have trouble with your ears. But that does not present a difficulty; you can come by boat. It is only a short distance to Nakhodka. Presumably you are all right in a boat?"

While they were joking about seasickness, Fumihiko realized that he could even visit Europe if he took the Trans-Siberian Railway across Russia. Meanwhile, the noise continued in the next room, with his daughter's voice the loudest of all.

"Sometime soon we must have a farewell party for you— Canna and I, that is. We can have it here. Canna and I will do the cooking."

Khukin thanked him for the suggestion and asked him to apologize to Canna for having to stop her skating lessons. He said he'd get in touch again once his schedule was worked out, then hung up.

In the next room someone was playing a guitar. As he listened, Fumihiko found himself thinking that once the big project he was currently working on was over, he, too, perhaps might change his job.

There are four events in women's gymnastics: the floor exercise, the vault, the uneven parallel bars and the balance beam. Right now I'm working on my program for the next champion-

ships. Normally we work on the four different events together, but for the past two or three days I've been concentrating on the balance beam, trying to get the most important bit right.

To learn any difficult move on the balance beam, you first draw a line four inches wide on the mat and practice on that, using it as a substitute for the actual beam. Once you can do the move without going outside the line too much you do the same thing on floor boards. Then you use a beam that's only about eight inches off the floor. Finally you do it on a proper beam and practice till you've got it absolutely right.

What I'm doing at the moment is a backward somersault with a twist. The key to keeping your balance on the beam is to keep the center of your body in a perfectly straight line above the beam. As long as you do that, it isn't all that hard to move up and down it. If there's a twist involved, though, you have to go off-center, which makes it all a lot tougher. A backward somersault with a twist isn't too hard to do on the mat, but when you're on a beam four feet high and you've only got a strip of wood four inches wide to land on and the landing has to be perfect, then you've got real problems.

Because I'd made good progress on the low beam our coach decided I should go on the high one today. His name is Yanai. He watched me on the low beam for a while, then said, "All right, Takatsu, let's give it a try." All the others stopped practicing and gathered around. The tallest of them, Kamizaki, who's also pretty strong, stood on one side of the beam with the coach on the other, so that there'd be someone to support me if something went wrong—if my foot slipped, for example.

So I get up on the beam. At this stage, I have to do the somersault separately. When I've learned to do it from a stationary position, I can fit it into an actual program and learn how to combine it with a number of other moves.

Probably the biggest hurdle on the high beam isn't so much the move itself as your fear of the height. Things that are almost no problem on the mat can be really tough up there.

I get up on the beam, close my eyes and make sure I've got my balance. I take three short steps backward, then launch. As I float in the air I start to twist from the hips. Your entire body has to make a perfect 360° turn, otherwise when your feet land there'll be no bar for them to land on. My body turns lightly and smoothly. It doesn't feel so much that I'm turning as that I'm the still center of a universe that's spinning in all directions. I'm now set free from the ground, from all the world around me, touching nothing but air as I slowly turn.

I'm aware of my hair, tied up in a ponytail, dancing in space. The fluorescent lights up on the ceiling flick their tails across my field of vision. My elbows are tucked neatly into my sides and my movement is quite steady. It's all right—my feet are going to land squarely on the beam. I feel it. It's all right.

I'm sitting on Diplodocus's head. Bathed in the afternoon sunlight, my Dippy lumbers through the wood. Dippy knows I'm there. That's why he never shakes his head, although I wouldn't fall off if he only shook it a bit.

Dippy sometimes takes a branch full of leaves from a nearby tree into his mouth, strips the leaves off with his long, narrow teeth and eats them. That's the time when he moves his head about the most, and it's pretty scary. When he opens his mouth wide and thrusts his head in among the branches of a willow tree, I get pushed right in among the leaves as well. Then Dippy closes his mouth and pulls his head back, and I get a really rough brushing from the leaves, while the branches bend and the trunk twists and there's a great crackling sound as lots of twigs get pulled off. But the leaves are all in his mouth, and he slowly swallows them *before walking off to another tree.*

Because I'm perched up on his head, I can see a really long way. There's a line of hills far off beyond a series of woods, so distant they're a hazy purple. To the south I can see a river glittering in the sun. Behind us is the town. In the bright rays of the sun the air above the town seems somehow cloudy.

Dippy is slowly moving north. South across the river there's a wood of acacia trees. Dippy really loves acacia leaves, but today he's not going there because of me. He moves with his back turned to the sun. The sun feels warm on my back.

As we go north the trees start to change. I've never been this far north before. Then I notice we're in a forest of scaly trees. Scaly trees are very tall, with long, long trunks, and right at the top the branches and leaves open like an umbrella. The bark on the trunk has the same pattern as a fish's scales. The leaves are like a fern's; in fact the tree belongs to the same family as ferns.

Dippy goes on eating away at those strange leaves. Because it's a very tall tree even Dippy's mouth can't reach to where the really thick foliage is, so he stands up with his front paws against the trunk, like a dog jumping up on his master, and stretches out his neck. I have to hang on tight to make sure I don't tumble off.

We've walked a long way into this wood and it's turned quite cold. I put on the sweater I've brought with me. When I look down I can see something white floating and swirling about Dippy's feet. It's mist, which must have flowed down here from farther north. The mist is slowly spreading through the lonely forest. It's heavier than air, so the effect is like floodwater rising, gradually covering the trunks of the trees and Dippy's lower body.

At last the forest of scaly trees comes to an end and we're out on a plain again. The mist has grown deep and thick, and when I turn around I can't see Dippy's back at all. Only his long, tapering head stands out above the swaying sea of fog. And there, right on top of that head, is me, in a world without a trace of color in it now.

I watched her from a little way off. I watched the girl sitting there alone on the head of the ambling diplodocus, swaying her body about cheerfully in time with the movements of that long neck. I knew it was me I was watching, from somewhere separate.

The fog got even thicker. No scaly trees were visible behind them now, no umbrella-shaped branches. Then even Dippy's long neck and the girl riding on him grew vague, their outlines fading. A gust of wind stirred up the fog and they vanished into that white darkness. Another gust blew the fog apart and for a while showed me their faint shadows.

But the me that rode on Diplodocus was gradually fading altogether from sight. I knew as I watched that what I was doing was saying goodbye to myself, that I would now become a different me. I strained my eyes to see into the fog, trying to catch sight of myself as I went away.

Diplodocus ambled on, with me still riding him, and finally disappeared into the fog forever. I waved my hand one last time to a Dippy and a self I couldn't see, then turned around and walked back toward a wood, one where I'd been before, a wood of willow trees.

UPLINK

The Islander could carry nine passengers, but he was the only one on board. The other seats had been taken out anyway, to allow the plane to be packed tight with a cargo of cardboard boxes full of food and medical supplies, two sacks of mail, and an assortment of batteries, stationery, clothing and other sundries.

He sat in the copilot's seat on the right. After they had taken off, he looked down at the rapidly receding land, at the sea, and then up at the sky. It was late afternoon, but the sky was still clear, a thin, pale blue. Buffeted by the air currents, the light plane bounced and yawed constantly.

"You've got plenty on board," he remarked loudly to the pilot when the exchange with the control tower was over.

"They haven't been able to get a boat to the island for a while now. Anything urgent has to be taken by plane. Naturally, the authorities aren't too happy about how much all this is costing. I'm doing all right out of it, but I've still got more than I can handle."

"What's wrong with the boats?"

"The wind ..." But the roar of the engine nearby and the whine of the propeller churning the air outside drowned out the rest of his words.

"What?"

The pilot turned to face him and shouted:

"It's the west wind. It won't stop blowing. The harbor faces due west and when the wind's in that quarter it can't be used.

Big waves come right into the harbor and boats can't dock. A strong west wind always blows round about this time, but for some reason it won't seem to die down this year. They can't get the fishing boats out, and some people are having trouble making ends meet. Everyone's having trouble, in fact."

"I get it," he shouted back.

It was exhausting trying to talk above the engine noise, so after that they hardly spoke and he just sat there looking at the instrument panel or the distant clouds, which he quite enjoyed. Now and again the control column in front of him moved slowly backward or forward in response to the pressure of the pilot's hand.

After they'd been flying for about forty minutes the pilot pointed ahead and said:

"Look. You can just begin to see it."

At first, the island was merely a black line above the water. As they approached, however, its shape became clear: long and narrow, like the back of some huge animal submerged in the sea. The central mountain range was its backbone. You could make out the barrier reef surrounding it some distance out to sea, where waves were breaking in white crests.

"It's lucky they built the runway from east to west. If it'd been north–south you'd never be able to get a plane down with a crosswind like this."

They circled the island, flying over the runway to make sure it was free of any obstructions, then landed from the east into the teeth of the wind and the blinding glare of the late afternoon sun. As *The Islander* taxied toward the plain-looking terminal building, its fuselage shook and trembled with the force of the gusts.

As soon as he stepped out of the plane, the hot, humid wind seized hold of him, ruffling his short-cropped hair, squirming and fluttering inside his clothes, and tugging at his hands and legs. It certainly didn't feel like six o'clock in the evening. He felt heavy and tired, as if immersed in a lukewarm bath, and with each breath his lungs filled with muggy air.

There was no one at the airfield. The pilot was unloading the cargo, so he went around to his side of the plane and carefully took down the case containing the measuring device he'd held on his lap during the flight. He placed it gingerly on the ground, then looked about him, wiping the sweat from his forehead with his hand. What had happened to the person who was supposed to meet him? He'd been to several places in the region, but this was his first time on the island, which lay some hundred and thirty miles from the mainland.

Walking a short way from the pile of cargo which the pilot was still unloading, he noticed two vehicles, a car and a truck, coming over a low rise toward the airfield.

The pilot saw them too.

"People around here tend to take things pretty easy," he said.

When the vehicles finally arrived, a young man got out of the car and came up to him. He was smaller than average, with a chirpy sort of manner.

"Sorry I'm late. I run the Works Department here. I've been told to give you any assistance you might need," he announced loudly.

"Glad to meet you," the visitor said, and briefly introduced himself. "These two things are mine. I'll take care of this gadget, but the suitcase only has personal belongings in it, so you can bash it about as much as you like."

The young man, whose name apparently was Karaki, laughed at this in a voice that showed a complete indifference to the heat and the wind.

The visitor waved goodbye to the pilot, who was now helping the other driver load the cargo onto the truck, and got into the car.

"You'll be spending tonight in town," Karaki told him. "The weather station is some way outside town and I'll take you there tomorrow."

"So you're normally in charge of the station?"

"Well, sort of. I mean, I only really take a quick look around it occasionally. This is just a routine inspection, is it?"

"That's right. I wasn't told there's anything that needed repairing. Hell of a wind, isn't it?"

"Yes. If it doesn't die down soon we're going to be in real trouble. It's the prevailing wind at this time of year, but it's been going on much longer than it should. The main problem is that the harbor's out of action," he said, confirming what the pilot had already said.

Hibiscus bushes grew along the road into town, their branches and pink flowers whipping about in the wind. The fields were dotted here and there with houses, each one surrounded by a grove of dark green trees with very thick-looking leaves, which presumably served as a windbreak.

The town center consisted of some twenty shops and public buildings lining both sides of the main street, a modest-looking hotel, and two hundred or so houses round about. Each house stood on a large, wooded plot, quite separate from its neighbor. Looked at closely, they were an odd mixture of what must have been the original kind of building here—tile reinforced with white stucco—and clapboard structures that reminded him of a Wild West movie set. He was struck by the weirdness of the place, the way the walls had been scrubbed clean by the constant friction of the wind. The hotel itself was a two-storied affair of white-painted wood, although most of its ground floor seemed to be taken up by a supermarket.

The moment he stepped out of the car, he was caught by a cloud of dust. He stood still with his eyes closed as the wind swirled through his hair.

In front of the supermarket was a square containing a single tall sago palm, at least twelve feet high. Some women had gathered under the tree, doing nothing in particular, apparently. He glanced at them, assuming they must have come to do their shopping, then noticed that none of them was carrying anything. The faces that were turned his way were all dark, with rather striking eyes. A few of them looked exotic, even foreign, yet they didn't seem out of place so much as just another aspect of the group. The women stared so hard he began to feel uncomfortable. He found himself exaggerating the care he took unloading his precious instrument from the car.

"I've told the hotel about you. They've got a restaurant, so I suggest you take your meals there." Karaki rattled off advice as though reciting something by heart. "There's probably no beer left, and there won't be any more till the wind lets up and the next boat comes in. There's a local liquor made from sweet potatoes, which they'll get out if you ask for it. It's not all that bad, in fact. I'll call for you at nine o'clock tomorrow. Actually, I live just down the road, so I'll leave the car here; the key's in it if you want to use it. You can go for an evening drive if you get bored, though there's nowhere much to go. Here, I'll take your bags up."

This was delivered in what seemed like a single breath. He then picked up the suitcase and strode off toward the hotel entrance at the side of the supermarket. The visitor followed with the other case.

It occurred to him that the young man was probably not a local, and came from the mainland or even farther away. There was something in his bearing that set him off from the other islanders—the old people trudging down the street, the middle-aged fishermen lounging about and the children who darted across the road to vanish around corners. It wasn't a question of how slowly they spoke or gestured, compared with Karaki, either, but more a matter of rhythm, a difference of key.

An ordinary wind dies down at dusk, but this one continued throughout the night. Forgetting Karaki's recommendation about the local liquor, he went straight back to his room after a quick dinner in the hotel restaurant. He didn't much feel like going for a drive. There was no air conditioning in the room and no chance of opening a window. The windows were clearly made to be opened—they were even firmly fitted with insect screens —but he only had to push one open an inch to find a howling gale coming in.

As he listened to the rattle of the shutters he wondered why there was a hotel of this kind on the island at all. Everything about it suggested it had been requisitioned by the Occupation forces after the war and hadn't changed since. The toilets and baths were all Western-style, as was the cooking in the restaurant and the insistence on knives and forks. The vegetables served with the meat had been the inevitable sweet potatoes, but they had a buttery taste and were stone cold; the label "glacé" presumably indicated aspirations toward French cuisine. Even the authentically Japanese miso soup wasn't served in small drinking bowls but had to be scooped up genteelly from a plate with a spoon. To cap everything, the rice was dry, not sticky. All this had been served by a small, elderly waitress who was so silent as to be almost mute. He had tried addressing a few words to her, but she merely nodded and mumbled something. It seemed likely that she was doing the cooking herself, in the inner recesses she disappeared into from time to time, bringing out each dish as it was done. There were no other customers.

In the dim light of the lamp, he thought about the work he was supposed to do the next day and the order in which he should do it, then glanced over a few instruction manuals. Most of the unmanned weather stations he visited were linked up with the local telephone exchange by cable, although there were cases of stations located so far off in the hills that communication had to be established via special microwave transmission. But this was the first place he'd come across where everything was sent directly to a communications satellite. Wiping the sweat off his forehead with a towel, he realized a little ruefully that he was looking forward to the following day with much the same feelings as a child with a new toy.

He was just finishing his breakfast of bacon, eggs, bread and coffee the next morning when Karaki arrived.

"Good morning!" the latter said in the same absurdly cheery voice. "I'll be spending the whole day with you."

"Don't you have anything else to do?" he asked, trying not to make the question sound too pointed and offering him some coffee.

"No. As long as nothing actually breaks down I've always got plenty of time on my hands. And modern machines hardly ever do break down. You don't even have to oil most of them any more. So I just sort of wander about and check them over every once in a while."

"What sort of machines are you talking about?"

"Oh, just about any kind. The ones that matter most are the pumps for the water system. Then there are the machines they use in the offices at the town hall, plus three cars and a bulldozer. I also keep an eye on the weather station and the airfield. I'll even mend things like an electric toaster if I'm asked. The tele-phone exchange doesn't need any sort of maintenance, and there's another guy who looks after the power station."

"Might be a good idea to think of harnessing wind power here," the visitor said, listening to the roaring sound outside. He had only been on the island thirteen hours or so and most of those he'd spent asleep, but he was already sick to death of that constant noise.

"You're absolutely right," Karaki replied evenly, as if he scarce-ly noticed it.

The unmanned weather station was two miles away by car and the whole way there Karaki kept up a flow of chatter, like someone used to having not enough to do.

"It's like living in a different world here—even a different age. I wasn't sure what to make of it when I arrived. There's not much going on; they grow sweet potatoes and sugar cane and they fish out there beyond the reef. They also keep a few pigs, and the women do some weaving. Still, it's not all behind the times—some of it's weirdly up-to-date, a mixture of the good old days and something much more like the American way of life than anything they've got on mainland Japan."

"Like that hotel?"

"Exactly. The manager used to live in America. For decades now, people have been in the habit of leaving the island and going, not somewhere close by, but way overseas. Some of the old people still occasionally use the Spanish they picked up in Mexico or Bolivia, places like that. Sometimes you even find them celebrating these feast days that only meant something in some weird little corner of the world. And there are quite a lot of kids with mixed blood in them—you can easily tell—but they seem to fit in perfectly well here."

"Good for them," he replied, looking out the window at the

gently rolling fields of sugar cane. That probably accounted for the way some of those women outside the hotel yesterday had looked.

"Maybe so," said Karaki, though he sounded doubtful. "And then the houses are a funny jumble of styles," he went on after a pause. "People come back to the island with a bit of money saved, wanting the kind of places they've seen in the country they've just been in. Some of them worked as carpenters or builders over there, so they know how to put up a Western-style house. They do it in no time. That's why the town has that crazy look about it. Lots of people still emigrate; it's normal for the adults to go abroad. In fact I get the impression you don't really count around here if you haven't had any experience of foreign life. I don't seem to, anyway."

So that's what was bothering Karaki. Now that he'd figured it out, he began to find these gripes of his almost amusing. He could just imagine how, as a local civil servant fresh out of college, Karaki must have thought he was in for a nice, easy life when he was posted to this island. Here he was, a technician, someone for these islanders to admire and pay attention to. But none of the island's machines broke down and the local girls wouldn't even look at him. He was in limbo, drifting aimlessly. One was almost tempted to feel sorry for him.

The weather station stood on a small bluff above the sea, in quite extensive grounds enclosed by a fence and surrounded by fields of sugar cane extending as far as the eye could see. The wind, which was blowing much harder here than in the low-lying town, slammed into him as soon as he got out of the car.

The main building was built of reinforced concrete, but around it were a number of old-style, slatted wooden stands housing measuring instruments. The wind gauge was mounted high up on a steel tower. On the lawn there were remote-sensor rain gauges, a nephelometer to measure the degree of cloudiness, and a television camera inside a plastic dome. And in one corner was the parabola antenna that was used to make direct relays to the communications satellite 22,500 miles away. The wind gauge was spinning around at a tremendous rate.

"Where's the reflector for that visibility meter?"

"The what? Oh, the reflector. It's on top of the steel tower over in that field."

"I don't suppose you get any fog on this island."

"Fog? Well, there hasn't been any since I've been here …"

"That's what I would have thought. So how come they've given us a laser visibility meter?"

"Yes, that does seem odd."

"Anyway, let's start with the antenna."

"Ah, that doesn't belong to the weather station. It's the telephone company that's responsible for it."

"I know, but I was asked to take a look at it while I'm here. It's only a matter of checking azimuth alignment and elevation. I don't imagine anything needs doing, so I'll just check it out with the circuits still on. With this kind of wind blowing, it could get pushed out of line and then it wouldn't be any use to anyone, would it?"

The antenna was, in fact, pointed in the right direction, at the satellite high up over Indonesia. There were no problems with the receiver, and the backup machines were all in order. A motion check revealed nothing unusual.

Battling against the wind, they walked toward the main building which housed the station's central computer, among other machinery. He opened the front door with the key he'd been given and closed it firmly as soon as Karaki was inside. The air conditioning was working so well it was almost chilly. This was for the machines' benefit, of course, but they too were grateful for it.

"All I'll have time for today is the uplink."

"Eh?"

"It means the devices that send out data from here. This place is linked up with central office via the satellite, right? It collects meteorological information under various headings, sorts it out, memorizes it, then transmits it on the appropriate circuit at a fixed time. That's what's called 'uplink.' At the same time, it can also receive instructions from central office. This lets it make ad hoc measurements, check particular functions, change over to backup machines, shift the TV camera's position, operate the zoom or whatever. All that is referred to as 'downlink.'"

Karaki's eyes shone as he listened to this barrage of technical know-how. The poor guy was obviously bored out of his mind on this island.

"Of course, the concept of 'up' and 'down' only makes sense relative to the satellite. From the standpoint of central office it's the other way around, but for simplicity's sake when the station sends out information it's called 'up.'"

As if to underline this point he sat down in front of the computer and typed out a message to central, telling them he was about to carry out a routine check on this station and would be switching off the communication circuits for a while. A reply came back immediately, acknowledging the message and giving the go-ahead.

He proceeded to disconnect the machines from the computer one by one and test each of them carefully to ensure there wasn't even the slightest malfunction. All the necessary tools and maintenance equipment were kept at the station, except for the ultrasensitive measuring device he'd brought with him —a very recently calibrated model. Checking the seismometer with this took the most time and effort. Karaki stood next to him while all this was going on, observing everything and trying hard not to distract him with questions.

As he was inspecting the rain gauge he said:

"It's easy enough to make a machine to measure rainfall. The real problem is getting it to tell you if it's actually raining or not. Once some rain has accumulated in a flask any machine can work out how much there is, but at the stage where only a few drops have started falling you need something really sensitive to figure it out."

"Yes, I can see that," Karaki said, paying close attention.

"Even *we* find it hard to tell the difference between rain mist and just plain mist. Another problem is differentiating between rain and sleet—not that it's relevant here, of course."

"Can a machine do that?"

"Some can. However, we don't yet have a machine that can work out cloud types. The cloud altimeters they have at large airports can tell you how low the cloud cover is, but it has its work cut out to interpret cloud type from cloud shape. It's a question of image analysis, you see."

"Then how do you do it?"

"Use the device we've got outside here, the TV camera. It's pointed at the sky; it's only a matter of changing the lens. Take off the normal fisheye lens and use one that shows cloud detail. The head position's adjustable. There's no need for it to take in the whole sky all the time; when necessary, it can be used to look at clouds."

Karaki looked a bit like the dog listening to His Master's Voice. There had to be some way of getting rid of him for a while.

"Look, I wonder if you wouldn't mind doing me a small favor?"

"Yes, sure," he said enthusiastically.

"It's that reflector for the visibility meter. You said it was up on the bluff, didn't you?"

"That's right. On the steel tower in the field."

"If the glass gets dirty there can be a slight deterioration in performance. The machine is self-adjusting, so the data's being transmitted all right, but I'm beginning to think it would be better to give the reflector a good cleaning instead of tinkering about here. Would you mind doing that for me?"

"Of course not," Karaki replied, heading straight off with a cloth in his hand.

The visibility meter had a base line of just over half a mile, so the reflector would be in the middle of that. A quarter of a mile there and the same back, plus the time it took to climb up and polish it: the whole thing would take him a good thirty minutes. At least it was a bit of useful work for him to do, he thought, as he watched him running through the field of wind-blown sugar cane. Karaki was so keen he'd probably be back once a week from now on to give it the same treatment.

Lunch consisted of sandwiches Karaki had brought with him. Apparently he'd gone to some trouble to get the hotel to make them. He sat on the floor next to the computer and opened the paper wrapping.

"I've brought these as well, though I'm afraid they're still a bit warm," Karaki said, producing a bag he'd stood in front of the air-conditioning outlet. There were two cans of beer inside.

"I thought you said there was no beer left on the island?"

"This is from my own private store. For personal consumption only. I've just about reached rock bottom, though."

"Don't you mind? I mean ..."

"No, go ahead. After all, the wind's got to stop sometime, and the first boat in will be loaded with it."

"Depending on the wind."

They sat quietly for a while eating and drinking. The sandwiches—egg and cucumber on fresh, soft bread—were surprisingly good.

"I wonder if there'll ever come a time when they'll be able to do something about the weather," said Karaki.

"You mean change it by human intervention?"

"Yes."

"Not very likely. We're talking in terms of energy on a totally different scale. We can foul up little corners of it with smog and acid rain, but the whole thing is infinitely more complex."

"Is it?"

"First of all, we still don't understand what actually causes the weather. We know that a rise of just one degree in mean temperature can make a huge difference in, say, crop yield in cereals, but we haven't a clue really about the complex changes that have to take place in order to produce that rise."

"But what about all the data we're getting from all the monitoring that's going on?"

"All the monitoring only covers a fraction of the whole. The human race may be very full of itself, interfering with various aspects of nature all over the globe, but there's not a thing we can do about the weather. All we can do is struggle along after it, trying to find out what's been happening. We can't even be sure we're going to get tomorrow's forecast right."

"Still, by using really high-speed computers ..."

"Use as big a computer as you like, you still can't accurately simulate the world's overall weather. And if you can't forecast the movements of something, there's no way you're going to even begin to control it."

"Hopeless, is it?"

"Absolutely, and a good thing, too. You know, I didn't get started in meteorology because I had this burning desire to serve mankind by producing more reliable weather forecasts. The way I see it, the weather's something you observe, not something you manipulate. It's a completely one-sided affair, something undergone, something endured; we're at its mercy—all of us, equally. And I like it that way. I like the idea that nature isn't something we can do as we like with."

"That's what you think?"

"That's what I think."

Perhaps he'd overemphasized this point, because Karaki looked rather disheartened afterward and was uncharacteristically silent, remaining so throughout the afternoon.

Servicing the machines and checking the computer's uplink program took him until five o'clock. He then drove the car back to town, making leisurely progress along the undulating road through the fields of sugar cane. Karaki, saying he had to drop in at the town hall to submit his report before going home, got off at the second crossing before the hotel, leaving him to drive on by himself.

Since he'd left all the tools and equipment at the weather station, he had nothing to carry except the car key, which he took with him when he got out, though he didn't bother to lock up. The wind was as strong as ever, lashing the leaves of the sago palm about in front of the supermarket. Standing in its fitful shade was the same group of women, all staring at him just as they'd done the day before. He wondered what they could find so interesting about someone who was merely a visitor from outside, and glanced briefly in their direction. They were huddled shoulder to shoulder, except for one of them, who had taken a step forward. Her hair was done up on top of her head and she wore a print dress with a loud floral pattern. She looked about thirty, though somehow she gave the impression she could have been much younger. Her face was lowered, but she kept her eyes fixed on him; it was a sharp, almost fierce look, much bolder than any of the women behind her, who seemed to be just backing her up or perhaps encouraging her to go up to him.

He walked past with his eyes averted, the way one might pass a group of street kids hanging about on a corner. He would have liked to return the woman's gaze, but he'd just finished a full day's work and wasn't up to that kind of encounter. Inside the hotel lobby he turned and looked back at the whole square. From there the styles of the various buildings looked more muddled than ever, inspiring the general feeling that one might be anywhere, or nowhere. The woman was still staring at him, but the group behind her had dispersed.

The hotel staircase gave a different creak at each step. The upstairs hallway was in semidarkness and the lights weren't on in the dining room. There was no one at reception. He took down his key and went to his room, where he picked up a fresh towel before going for a shower.

An hour later, as he was eating his dinner attended by the same elderly and silent waitress, a small old man wearing a checked cotton shirt and corduroy trousers appeared from somewhere inside the kitchen and slowly approached. His face was heavily wrinkled, but he walked firmly enough. He stopped at his table, and his eyes glittered as he spoke.

"Ah, so you're the one who's come to fix the weather. I was

away yesterday, so I apologize for not being here to meet you when you came. I'm the hotel manager."

This, presumably, was the man who had spent a while in America. His guest had his mouth full and could only nod a greeting in return as he went on chewing. The old man lowered himself into the chair opposite with a succession of grunts and a final sigh of relief.

"Well, how's the weather getting on then?"

What the old man had said earlier suddenly sank in.

"I haven't actually come to fix the weather, I'm here to check the machinery that monitors the weather."

"Have you, now? Just the machinery? So you're not going to put a stop to this wind for us?"

"Sorry. It can't be done. There's nothing any human agency can do."

What did he mean by fixing the weather? Did this old man have some kind of blind faith in modern science? Was he going senile? Or did his mind work on a different plane entirely?

The waitress brought a dish of some soft, milky-looking stuff and put it in front of the manager. It seemed they were to dine together.

"I hope you'll excuse me, but I thought I might as well join you for my bowl of porridge. It's the only kind of thing I can eat nowadays ... So, as far as the weather goes, there's nothing any human agency can do?" he repeated, transferring a spoonful of porridge to his mouth.

"You'd be better off asking the gods." The remark, come to think of it, was rather out of character for him.

"No, no, mustn't do anything like that," said the old man vigorously, looking him straight in the eye. "The gods aren't like that. They can't be asked to do just anything we want, you know."

"Oh really?"

"Listen. When I was young, in Mexico, there was this friend of mine, and he came from a very old family. In those parts that means very old—been there for a thousand, maybe two thousand years. What you might call the aristocracy of that part of the world. Of course, at the time he was just a wildcatter, like me—we were in the same game together."

The old man looked up at the ceiling as if he were gazing at some distant place, and chuckled.

"It's something he once told me. He said there was a god everywhere something important was going on. You found gods all over the world, in the stars, in everything that mattered. So they didn't have time to listen to the little things we humans asked for. When I heard that, I figured it was important, so I made sure I remembered it. The gods are very busy; they've got important work to do."

"Well, yes, I suppose that's only to be expected." One might as well humor the old fool, he decided.

"That's what the old Mexican gods are like, anyway. People ask them to do this and that. I'm sick, make me better. Help me get that woman, help me get that man. And then, when they've got them, it's oh, help me have a child, that kind of thing. And it's all wrong. They shouldn't ask things like that. There's such a thing as order in the heavens, and that's what the gods are looking out for. That's their job."

Outside the window the wind still howled. The ceiling fan was spinning but the dining room was hot and close, and beads of sweat stood out on his forehead. The manager's face, however, looked perfectly cool as he went on eating his steaming porridge.

"Still, you know," the old man added, looking at his face intently, "I reckon something ought to be done about this wind.

But you say you can't fix the weather? Can't do a thing about it?"

"That's right. Not a damn thing."

"Well, that figures. It's a pity those gods don't have any spare time, though, you know? If they'd just pay a little bit of attention sometimes to what people say. Just occasionally. Just listen a bit every now and again."

The old man focused that intent gaze on him again and then laughed.

"Now, if we had some way of getting in touch with them, that would be a start."

But even an uplink that could describe existing conditions with absolute precision couldn't begin to convey ideal conditions—how we wanted things to be. The satellite simply received information and relayed back instructions. It was all one-way traffic, really. Whether it was the Central Meteorological Office that lay on the other side of the satellite or the ancient Mexican gods, the satellite's function remained the same.

"If there was only a way, that would be something," the manager said again. He seemed to have finished his porridge while he'd been talking. "Well, I guess I've been making a nuisance of myself. Can't be any fun listening to an old man's nonsense." He then stood up slowly, saluted Indian fashion with one raised hand and plodded off.

The other watched him go in silence.

When he got back to his stifling room, he found he couldn't think of anything to do. It was too early to go to bed, there was no television, and he'd brought nothing to read. He ought to have got hold of some of the local rotgut, but couldn't be bothered to go back to the lobby in search of the old man or the crone who seemed to be his helpmate, just for the sake of a

drink. He didn't want to get entangled in any more useless conversations, either. His head was full of the pinging of communications satellites and measuring devices; incongruous images of
ancient Mexican gods and aristocratic Indians wandered amid
the din; and through and above all these sounds and faces the
wind roared on.

He sat in the antique armchair for a while, trying to clear his
head. The chair was of a curious and complex design, like something brought from the Wild West a hundred years ago, and
wasn't very comfortable. It seemed to have been made for people of a different build. Still, he sat in it for quite a long time,
doing nothing and thinking nothing, when he suddenly remembered he'd left his cigarettes in the car. These he needed.

After another quick shower, he went downstairs as quietly as
he could, wearing the beach sandals that served as slippers, and
pushed through the hotel door. An enormous moon hung in
the sky. The sago palm stood silhouetted against it, its long
leaves whipping and rattling in the gale.

As he moved toward his car he saw someone standing there
motionless in the moonlight. It was the woman he'd noticed
that afternoon, the one who had stood a step in front of the
others and stared unwaveringly at him. He had no sense of this
being odd or suspicious in some way, and he approached her.

"Good evening," he said, and she bowed her head slightly in
reply. "The moon's out," he added, nodding at the sky.

She didn't look at the moon but at his face, and then came
slowly toward him. He realized that her hair, which had been
coiled on top of her head during the day, now hung softly down
her back. It was abundant, slightly wavy, and tousled by the
wind.

She stopped in front of him and stared into his eyes. Her
own were black and glittering. As he returned their gaze he felt

they were eyes he knew, eyes seen in some very distant, very special memory. But he couldn't place it. Perhaps it was a memory of his childhood, or even beyond that, generations before he was born. Perhaps it wasn't a human memory at all, but came from a setting predating human history, when other species roamed the surface of the earth, unknown creatures that watched and tracked each other.

Whatever it was, he found it hard to turn his eyes away. He looked her full in the face, but felt none of the self-consciousness he might normally have felt staring at a stranger. Her face was dark-skinned and round, the nose well formed, the lips full. She seemed to be wearing no makeup and looked at him without expression. Again he had the sensation of knowing this face. It wasn't simply one he happened to have seen yesterday and today, or one that had been imprinted on his mind in images or words he could recall, but a face he'd caught a glimpse of, brushing close past perhaps, on many occasions since his childhood. He remembered the eyes and the nose, a touch, a fragrance. If he heard her voice, he knew he would remember that too. And he felt suddenly peaceful, as calm and comfortable as a cat dozing in the sun.

Still saying nothing, the woman took his arm. He felt his body succumbing to this gentle compulsion and, unresisting, began to walk with her. It seemed as natural as a tree putting out leaves. As he walked he knew he had done this before, that the roads they followed were familiar and that this woman meant more to him than any other. The feeling kept recurring, as if the memory that prompted it were a message being transmitted repeatedly from very far away, to soothe him and enable him to go on walking with her.

There was a scent in the air: the odor of her body, the pleasant smell of sweat, the blended fragrance of the white flower pinned above her ear, distant woods and the animals at rest in them. She no longer held his arm because it was around her waist, but she leaned slightly toward him, her back still straight and supple. The wind blew and the moon shone, and there was no one else around, though it could hardly have been very late.

The woman's house stood in the shadow of a large, unfamiliar tree. It was a small house; in the dim light it seemed the perfect size for a woman to inhabit modestly, alone, radiating comfort and repose.

She went in first, closing the door after him. The house consisted of one room, with a crude bed in one corner and a plain table and chair in the middle. He sat down on the chair, feeling the house shudder with each strong gust of wind. The woman knelt before him and passed her hands slowly over his. Reduced to a state of pure passivity, leaving everything now to her, he simply sat there, knowing that this was what he had to do, and that if he went on as he was doing now he would be safe and secure and everything would fall into place. The woman continued stroking his hands, and where her skin touched his he felt a pleasant warmth, a clarity, invade his body and flow through it like a current.

Abruptly, she stood up and crossed to the far side of the room. He watched her, vacantly observing the solid set of her shoulders and the straight line of her back, the hair that hung halfway down it, the sway of her sturdy thighs. He analyzed nothing but simply saw her as she was. He was still in thrall to the idea that she was actually there, that the body of the woman who meant most to him was also closest to him.

She came back almost at once, carrying a glass of water. He took it from her hand and drank. It was plain water, pure-tasting. He felt like some forest-dweller who at last finds the courage to climb down from his tree and go to the riverbank, watches the flowing water for a while, then finally puts his hand in to scoop it up and bring it to his lips. The way he imagined that river water tasting was how this water tasted to him now.

The woman stood in front of him and slowly took off her dress. She undid the buttons one by one, her back still straight, her eyes still fixed on his face, then drew her arms through the sleeves, removed the dress and with one hand laid it across the back of the chair. She had nothing else on. He placed the glass of water on the table and looked up at her where she stood about six feet away, facing him as if to show him her whole body, silently urging him to stand and approach her.

So he stood up. He walked toward her, noting the firm curves of her body, the dark skin, the full, heavy breasts. So this was what the woman was like, he thought, and immediately another thought followed: this was what all women were like and he was like all men. She stretched out her hand and unbuttoned his shirt, then took it off and stroked his chest. He pulled her gently toward him, catching the scent of her hair. Now, he realized, he no longer needed to be himself; he could be anybody now—it didn't matter who he was. There was only the scent of the woman's hair, the feel of her breasts pressed against his chest, the faint dampness of her perspiration and the hesitant movement of her hand below reaching for his nakedness. He felt himself being drawn into a different time scale.

The bed was right beside them. He held her by the shoulders, turning her slowly in that direction, and like a large tree quietly keeling over, they fell together on the bed. The woman's body was on top of his, and he willingly took her weight. She held his face in her hands, while her lips explored his shoulders and his neck and then were pressed on his. Yet there was something awkward and unaccustomed about her movements, as if

she weren't doing what she wanted to do but what she'd been
told she must do.

Then the storm broke. He realized that a great force was
running through him, but that somehow he wasn't tapping it
himself, nor was it flowing to the woman's body. His hands
sought and touched every inch of her; his tongue tasted every
cranny; but the person doing all this wasn't him. Her body was
heavy and powerful, warm and deep; from her skin, soon running with sweat, a strong odor arose, and her fingers held him
firm. His own hands traveled from her buttocks to her hands,
holding them down above her head. But it wasn't him doing
these things; he wasn't the one pinning her hands and it wasn't
his penis that entered between her thighs.

From that instant, he knew he had become a kind of offering. He was being used for something. His body and his mind,
and no doubt the woman's body and her mind as well, were
being offered to some existence much greater than the two of
them, some wholly different reality that radiated to every corner of the universe, something infinitely grand, remote and
unapproachable that did not ordinarily take part in human
affairs. He felt all this in the sense of huge, exhilarating surprise
that overcame him, in the surges of pleasure and strength he
was experiencing, in the changing postures their two bodies
assumed as each new and strange and stronger stimulus led to
further heights, and in the wondering realization that his body
was actually doing and feeling such things.

He pressed his eyes against the darkness of the woman's
breasts and shuddered at what he saw there. Deep in that darkness, lights gleamed and flashed and ran together. Dazzling
nebulae formed, filling his whole field of vision with sudden
brilliance. Then, just as suddenly, they faded, and a darkness so
deep it horrified him flowed back; and across it columns of

abstractions came in like waves and crashed against each other, locked in turmoil until one army was defeated and they drew apart again. But even while he watched he knew he wouldn't remember. Memory wasn't permitted. He was only allowed to look, not to understand. He would simply have to accept it all, along with the smell of her sweat, the harsh intake of her breath, her long hair entangled with his limbs, her continuing moans and cries.

As the storm of sensations went on, he became aware of something else. Various instructions were being conveyed through him; it appeared he was the medium for those signals that release great air masses or hold them in reserve or send them to merge with others or disperse, as required. He felt these signals as pulsations of energy that shook their two bodies every time they were emitted, the radiating energy forming numerous precise shapes with each pulsation. When that had happened a million, perhaps a billion, times, a complex sequence was achieved, a complete signal that only had to be transmitted once. At that moment he understood the entire sequence necessary for this one instruction to be sent and carried out, but a split second later he had forgotten it.

So, after a long, long time, it came to an end, for everything that had to be conveyed had been conveyed and they could both become themselves again. It was then, with a sense almost of reassurance, that he peacefully achieved emission. His overheated body cooled and calmly, one by one, the various functions it had performed now slowed and stopped.

When he awoke in the chilly dawn air the woman was sitting, still naked, on the chair by the bed, looking intently at him once again. He said nothing, but got up, took the clothes she handed him, put them on and went outside. She silently closed the door behind him. They had said nothing to each other. He knew the way back to the hotel; he wouldn't get lost. Still half asleep, he walked down the road.

Climbing the stairs to his room, he was overtaken again by the desire for sleep, but just before he fell into bed he recalled with a jolt of surprise what it was that had drawn him out of the hotel earlier that night. He'd gone to get his cigarettes. And yet, as he was only now remembering, he'd given up smoking five years ago. He hadn't left any cigarettes in the car. How could he have done? Right from the start, then, he had merely been used by something unknown as an instrument, a device. The thought was oddly comforting.

He was dragged out of a deep sleep by a knock on the door.

"Good morning! Are you up yet? It's Karaki! Good morning!"

Even that voice wasn't enough to drive away the wish to sleep that seemed to bind his head and face like a heavy bandage. Using both hands as if to drag the bandage off, he managed to sit up in bed and mumble some kind of answer. He got up, but the memory of the night before, of the woman's face and body and, vaguely, of that overwhelming physical experience, floated to the surface of his mind, so that he had to stand still for a moment beside the bed. Then he went to the door and opened it a fraction.

"Sorry. I overslept. I'll be down in a moment. Would you mind waiting in the car?"

"Okay." Karaki's tone was as cheerful as ever, and he clattered off down the stairs.

Realizing he'd slept in his clothes, which were now crumpled and creased, he stripped, washed his face and put on a fresh shirt and trousers.

The old man was standing there as he walked past the dining room.

"Nice morning."

"Good morning."

"How about breakfast?"

"I don't have time. I overslept, and I've got to finish my work in time to catch the afternoon plane."

"They certainly work you hard. But you're doing a great job," he said, looking toward the window, whose shutters were now open. "You know …"

"Yes?"

"Sometimes the gods do look our way. Just a quick look and only sometimes, but …"

"They do?"

"It's a question of going about it the right way, following the proper procedures."

He couldn't see what the old man was getting at, so he nodded briefly and ran down the stairs. Outside, the square was full of people. Children were scampering about, housewives and old men were standing in groups gossiping. They all seemed to be in the best of spirits. The place was certainly humming this morning, he thought to himself. It didn't seem to be a festival, though. Perhaps any place, even one like this, puts on a different face on market day.

He looked up at the tall sago palm. Then he noticed. The tree stood there quite straight and still. Not a leaf was stirring.

STILL LIFE

You shouldn't think that this world exists for your benefit. It isn't a box that contains you.

You and the world are like two trees standing together. Neither approaches the other; both grow erect.

You are aware that the splendid tree we call the world is beside you, and this makes you happy. But it may be that the world is barely concerned with you at all.

In any case, there is another, inner world. You could think of it as a vast interior twilight. Your mind inhabits the border between both these worlds.

What matters is the forging of links, the passing of messages between the outer world of mountains, people, factories and insects singing and the wide world within. Even while a distance is maintained between them, there should be a sense of worlds moving in unison or harmony.

Like looking at the stars, for example.

If a sense of harmony, or unison, is achieved, you'll find it much easier to get through the days. The need to waste mental effort on indifferent things will disappear.

You'll discover the taste of water. You won't irritate people so much, perhaps not at all.

Admittedly it's hard to look at the stars the right way, but the better you get at it the more you'll notice these effects.

And it's not just stars. Shallow, running streams, or a sudden shower of cicada song, would do just as well.

*

Talking of stars.

We were seated on stools at the bar, each with a glass of whiskey and a glass of water in front of us.

He held the glass of water in his hand and stared at it intently. He wasn't looking at anything in the water and he wasn't looking through the water at something else. He was simply gazing at the perfectly transparent liquid.

"What are you looking at?" I asked him.

"I was thinking I just might be lucky enough to see the Cherenkov effect."

"The what effect?"

"Cherenkov. It's when a corpuscle from outer space happens to collide with a water nucleus, emitting light. I was wondering if I might see that happen."

"You can see things like that happen, can you?"

"Well, this is a pretty small quantity of water. You wouldn't be likely to get the effect in this amount more than about once every ten thousand years. It's also a bit too bright in here. Probably couldn't see the flicker even if there was one."

"But you're still waiting for it?"

"A billion corpuscles, a billion minute particles of light, must fall into this glass every second. But the water nucleus is tiny. They almost never score a direct hit."

I couldn't tell from his tone of voice whether he was being funny or serious.

"With an amount of water measured in thousands or millions of tons, and in pitch darkness, you'd be able to see the flicker of light from time to time. But it's hopeless, probably, here."

When this conversation took place I actually didn't know him very well. We'd met at work and had an occasional drink together, chatting about nothing special, but that was it. I didn't even know where he lived. I was simply listening, not particularly attentively, to what he was saying in his usual near-monologue.

"Corpuscles, did you say?"

"Suppose that far out in space a star explodes. When that happens, countless tiny, virtually weightless corpuscles of light are hurled out to begin journeying for thousands of years through the universe. Some of them reach earth. When I say 'some,' I'm talking about billions arriving at this glass each second."

"From a star."

"Yes. It's best to think of things at a distance. And stars are the most distant things we know."

I felt as if I were looking down at myself from some far, high place. Inside my skull was a dark emptiness; countless corpuscles of light fell through my head and flickered in that darkness. What should have been the mere vacuum of my brain was somehow watching me as I expanded and spread out to the far corners of space. And beyond the immense silence was a man with a glass of water in his hand, gazing at the water.

The first time I went drinking with Sasai was on the evening of the day I made a major mess-up at the dye works. He must have noticed the way the manager was bawling me out, and decided to help by taking some of the blame himself. I invited him out for a drink afterward as a way of thanking him.

I should explain that the work being done in the dyeing shop when I was there was a three-stage process. The first stage took place in a large room with a number of enormous vats in it. This room always had a faint stench of acid floating about, and only regular staff worked there, not part-timers like myself and Sasai. Skeins of raw thread were hung on dozens of frames and lowered into the vats of dye. The color they were to be dyed was shown on coded job tickets sent from the design shop. For example, if the design shop wanted a dark blue with the faintest hint of purple and a slight sheen when woven, the ticket was marked 2557-SS, and so on. For the thread to turn out exactly the shade that had been ordered, tremendous care had to be taken with the temperature of the dye and the length of time the thread was exposed to it. It was tricky work that called for quite a lot of experience.

In one corner of this area was the color room, a small place with white walls. It was equipped with special lights and cases containing color samples, meaning that in theory one could always compare any piece of work with what was in there. Yet the room was hardly ever used. Someone might drop by from the design section now and again to watch what was going on, but such keenness wasn't much appreciated by the workers.

After the dye had taken and the skeins had been washed, they were put into a stainless steel device to drain. The part-timers' work started at that point and lasted until the material was passed over to the people in the drying room. There were twenty skeins in each bucket and ten buckets counted as one lot through the entire drying process. It was essential that one lot never got mixed up with another at the draining stage, as I'd been told over and over again on my first day. The fact was, though, that even if two lots carried the same code—2557-SS, say—there was always a slight variation in color after they'd been dyed. You couldn't tell them apart at this stage, but the difference became obvious once they'd been woven.

I knew all that, but on this particular day we were being rushed off our feet. Skeins kept coming out of the vats all looking the same color, the draining room was a chaos of activity, and one of the buckets I'd put neatly on the floor somehow got into a different lot. The space between the lines of buckets was quite narrow, and I think someone must have knocked the bucket to one side with his rubber boot as he walked through. Anyway, after I had dumped one lot into the machine, pushed the button and got started sorting the next lot, I realized there had been a mix-up.

Because of the pressure we were all under that day, the manager was more incensed by this than usual. He planted himself in front of me and shouted for a good five minutes, spitting and blustering until he finally lost his temper altogether, turning red in the face and waving his arms about.

"I ask you! Anything goes wrong, *I'm* the one who gets it in the neck. It's *me* who has to write out the report now. I know, I know—you're working your butts off for lousy pay—it brings tears to my eyes, it really does. But what the fuck d'you think you were doing getting the lots mixed up? How could anyone be so dumb?"

"I'm sorry, but I think I must have moved one of the buckets with my foot," somebody standing near us said. He spoke in a calm, low voice, and the manager, losing his stride for a moment, turned and looked at him.

"So it was you, was it, Sasai?—you're the one who did it."

Sasai was a quiet man who had taken a job at the dye works three months after me. He was only a part-timer too, and got the same salary I did. He seemed to be a little bit older than me. We'd exchanged greetings but never had much else to say to each other; in fact he never talked to anyone in particular, preferring to keep to himself and just get on with his work.

Now that the manager had two targets for his wrath, he gradually calmed down.

"Well, we can't do much about it now. When the lot's dry, you'll have to separate it out, and when your shift's over you'll have to take it to the weaving shop and tell them what's happened. Apologize as best you can. It'll have to be treated differently from the rest. Maybe it can be dyed again once it's been woven, or maybe they can use it the way it is. Anyway, that's for them to work out. Whatever they do, it's going to be sold off cheap, so do it again and you're fired. God knows how anyone can make a fuck-up of work like this—so damn simple you don't even have to think."

That was how I came to invite Sasai for a drink that evening, at a bar where I was something of a regular even though the place had almost nothing to recommend it. We had a bite to eat somewhere else first, then stopped in at the bar and started drinking. Everybody knows those quiet types who can become noisy, uncontrollable even, when they've had a drink or two, but Sasai remained his usual coolheaded self. He slowly emptied his glass, had it refilled, then just as methodically emptied it again.

We talked for a while about baseball, and then I described the scenery of an island in Southeast Asia I'd been to, and Sasai told me about some mountain you could apparently see from a high building in Tokyo and the way it showed the curvature of the earth. It was an odd subject, yet he talked about the mountain with a curious detachment—not like a dog lover talking up the cleverness of this or that species or a butterfly collector praising some rare specimen, but like a man casually mentioning a butterfly he'd happened to see during a walk in the mountains.

Since the pair of us appeared to be happy enough talking to each other, the girls in the bar went and sat with other customers and didn't give us another glance. We had very little to say about ourselves. Work wasn't even mentioned, despite what had happened that day; we were just two young men quietly drinking, discussing things quite removed from our everyday concerns.

Two days later Sasai called me over and told me he was quitting. He had no particular reason, he said; he just liked doing whatever came into his head, which was why he never tried to get a permanent job. In that respect he was like me. It was much easier to drift than put down roots. Sasai said a brief goodbye, then went back to his work. From the next day he was gone.

No noticeable changes took place in my way of life. I lived alone in a big house and turned up punctually every day for work. A girl I thought I was getting on all right with decided for no apparent reason to leave me. After this—although I don't think it was to console myself—I bought a secondhand car. It was a dull green with round headlights. But now that I had a car I found there were surprisingly few places I wanted to go to in it. On my day off I'd drive west down the expressway for four hours, then turn around at an interchange and drive four hours back.

About a month later, when I was still working at the dyer's, I had a phone call from Sasai. It was during the lunch break.

"Are you still working at that place?" he asked.

"Well, I still seem to be here," I replied.

He asked me to have a drink with him, and I agreed. He took me to a different place from the one we'd been to before; it was much quieter. The solitary bartender who was running it hardly said a word, though he smiled pleasantly enough.

"I wonder why they can't manage a bit more control over the colors," I said. After drinking for a while, we'd started talking about the job Sasai had quit and I was still doing.

"You mean so that the different lots would all be the same?"

"That's right. They're using the same threads, the same dye and the same fixer, and it all gets washed in the same way. There's no difference in either the temperature of the dye or the time the lots spend in the vats. Why do they all come out with these slight differences in color?"

"Because there's no such thing as a process that gives us absolute control over things. What happens in dyeing is that the molecules are really just doing whatever they want to do. All we're doing is giving them a helping hand."

"Only very small differences, but still different."

"Yes. And what we do is really just registering."

"Registering?"

"Men and women pair off at random, but the only thing the people in the Registry Office know about is the very last stage of the process. That's the only thing they care about, too. They can't interfere at some earlier stage and tell people what to do. All they know is that there are thousands of men and women in that bit of society they're responsible for, and a certain percentage of them have their marriages registered at the Registry Office. It's exactly the same with molecules. They join up with each other and we can see the result. If the Registry Office decided they'd like to get a hundred marriages a year all looking the same they wouldn't even know how to start."

"When I'd only seen clothes after they'd been made I used to think you could get exactly the color you wanted."

I was beginning to be aware that the place was unusually bright for a bar; you could have read a paperback in there quite easily. But there was no music, so people were talking quietly. One whole wall was covered by a photograph of a desert scene: gently undulating sand dunes stretched away to a distant horizon.

"There are probably a lot more places the human hand can't reach than we think there are," said Sasai. "The whole thing is like a shelf with some small object on it. The hand stretches up and tries to get hold of the object, but can't quite reach into the corner. And as long as you've got nothing to stand on you'll never be able to. There must be lots of cases like that."

"I suppose so," I said, struck by the metaphor.

He swallowed his drink slowly and went on:

"The interesting thing is that we know there's something left up there on the shelf, as if the shelf itself were transparent and we could see what was on it. It's the same with the dye. We can't get a consistent color, but we can see the differences very clearly. Which is pretty frustrating."

"And that's why the manager...?"

"Right. That's the real reason he got so angry that day. Deep down he's got this question constantly nagging at him: Why won't it all come out the same color? Then at times like that the frustration just boils over."

"He certainly went over the top that day, but he's really not so bad. You can always figure out what's going on inside his head."

"Well, he doesn't mince his words, I'll say that for him."

"I'm finding I really like working there. You threw in the towel pretty quickly, but I'm thinking of staying on for another year. Might even decide to try for a permanent job."

"You mean you like the atmosphere of the place?"

"It's not that so much. I think the dyeing itself is interesting. I know this is the opposite of what you've been saying, but I like the way the colors don't all come out the same. They ought to be more adventurous about it, though—mixing the dyes at random, changing the conditions all the time, then deciding how the stuff should be woven and what else could be done with it after they've seen the colors."

"So if you were the manager you'd never yell at the part-timers, you'd just keep busy experimenting with new colors all the time? When a really weird one appeared you'd be off to the design people with it in a flash. In other words, the exact opposite of the way things are done now."

"Probably. I think you can divide people into two categories: the ones who like those slight color variations and the ones who are irritated by them. I've been wondering whether I should learn something about applied science and try to become a specialist."

The bartender looked over at us and pointed at Sasai's glass, which was nearly empty. Sasai nodded and had it refilled with bourbon. He'd already had several.

"Are you serious?" he said, looking straight at me.

"No, not really," I admitted. "I'm always planning to do things; I've made lots of plans. If I had a thousand years to live I could do them all, starting at the top and working my way down the list. But since I don't, I need to be selective and give things a lot of thought."

"You could always not think. Like the colors. Decide it's an area where your hand can't reach and leave it all to chance."

I'd had quite a bit to drink myself, but I felt completely sober, right to the very center of my head.

"There are places the human hand can't reach," Sasai repeated. "Places you have to leave to the angels and just watch what happens. We can't change the way the stars are arranged. We can't create some pattern out of them that we might like better. That's why we get this sense of relief when we look at them. There's nothing to be changed. They're just the way they are."

"You mean Ursa Major wasn't put there to sponsor some new line of teddy bears?"

We spent the whole evening talking like this. And it wasn't just us. Everyone else in that bar appeared to be drinking quietly and talking in low voices about much the same sort of thing: the revolution of the earth, species of coconut trees, the use of tropical land. At least that's what I gathered from the scraps of conversation I overheard here and there. Meanwhile the silent bartender moved deliberately and with evident satisfaction among his customers, filling their glasses without a word.

Since I didn't have a thousand years to live, I never knew what to try my hand at. What should I be doing? All I could think of for the time being was to go on working where I was and see how things turned out. The idea of deciding now what I would be doing in ten years' time seemed so illogical to me I couldn't make up my mind about anything. Society certainly seemed to favor people who were decisive, but that couldn't be helped. I chose to carry on in uncertainty.

Sasai was a bit of a mystery. On the surface he seemed to be just like me, drifting from one temporary job to another with intervals when he did no work at all. He told me that he once went to the cinema twelve times in a single week. He'd go away for a few days and call me when he got back (in fact this was a period when we seemed to spend a lot of time drinking together). These trips of his were mostly in the Tokyo area, though from the way he spoke it sounded as if he never actually chose the places he went to. He simply arrived there.

Where he was quite unlike me was in the impression he gave of not having the slightest interest in looking for something worth doing. And it wasn't just a matter of doing nothing in particular; he seemed to have no enthusiasms either. Whenever we met he went on in the same harmless way about the same sorts of things, never revealing anything about himself, his family or anybody else. There was certainly no mention of any girlfriend.

Sometimes he gave me the feeling that he'd already found whatever it was I was still looking for. Yet when I tried to draw him out on it he would only say that he was simply letting the days go by, no more than that. Still, it was clear that, unlike me, he managed somehow to see the world whole.

That's what matters, after all: having an overall grasp of the truth. Partial truths aren't hard to come by. If a partial truth is enough for you, it's a simple matter deciding what to do with your life. But with people who have the urge to see things whole, you get cases like me—drifters, unable to decide anything.

Sasai had already decided. He wasn't confused; he saw quite clearly what he had to do. But what that was I didn't know and he didn't tell me. I began to think that perhaps it was something you couldn't tell people; or perhaps he was just waiting quietly and patiently for the right moment, confident that one day it would come.

The morning after I'd noticed the first hint of spring in the air, I took a day off from work and boarded a train that went south, following the coast. The train heeled over as it traveled along, compelled by the narrowness of the track to demonstrate the effect of centrifugal force, rather like a small boy on a bicycle.

I'd been in the habit of making this trip for some years now. I always went to the same place, on the same train, usually at the beginning of March. It all started years ago when I was struck by a name on the map: a place called Amezaki, or "Rain Point." I had a steady girlfriend at the time, so I went with her.

She looked at the map and said: "It must be a place where it's always raining and the ground is permanently damp."

"I don't see how there could be a place like that," I replied.

We got off the train, took a short bus ride, walked along by the sea for a bit and there it was: Rain Point. The weather had been cloudy in Tokyo, but here it was a fine, sunny day. The earth underfoot was perfectly dry. My girlfriend, who had brought a big umbrella with her, looked disappointed.

A sandy beach extended to the headland, almost as wide as a school playground but strewn with steep rocks, which made for hard but exhilarating walking. We sat on a rock just within range of occasional bursts of spray and ate the sandwiches she'd made. Across the bay we could see the chimneys of a thermal power station. In the middle distance, the gray shadow of a tanker passed.

The next year, on a Sunday in early March, I remembered that day and went again. This time I was alone. I had no sandwiches. It was much colder than the year before, and there were no ships on the sea. From the chimneys of the power station white clouds of smoke steamed into the air. But everything else—houses, terrain—remained unchanged.

So I got into the habit of going there every year, though I don't remember ever planning it that way. Sometime each March, when I was wondering what to do the next day, I would remember Amezaki. The habit formed itself. Some years a warm sun shone down and I would find myself sweating as I climbed the rocks; at other times I turned up my collar against the wind.

It never once rained at Rain Point. Mostly I went by myself but occasionally with someone else; one year, six of us made a noisy expedition there. Two people brought fishing gear, but didn't catch a thing. The rest of us got bored watching people fish for nothing, so we larked about until the anglers gave up an hour later and we all took the bus to a nearby fishing port. In a restaurant there we ate fish and drank until evening. It wasn't at all bad going to Amezaki in a crowd.

But during the year in question I went alone again, not even having a girlfriend to invite along. I thought there might be people about at the weekend, so I went on a weekday. Since I had a car now, I considered going in that, but decided in the end to stick to my usual routine and took the cheerfully leaning train. The day before had been warm, but today the temperature had dropped and the sky through the train window was cloudy, gray and heavy, like the inside of a faded circus tent.

I got off the bus on the west side of the small bay, where the headland started. A narrow track followed the coast, passing behind a hut used for storing nets and other fishing gear. The planks of the hut had been bleached almost white by the salt wind and cracks had opened up in them. It was all exactly as it had been each time I passed this way. Nothing had changed.

There was no wind at all, but it was cold. I followed the track through a stand of pine trees and out again into a small clearing with clumps of withered grass. The land was a bit marshy here and my shoes sank into the soft earth. Then the track wound among pines again and here the earth was bone dry and firm underfoot. I walked on and at last reached the beach with its scattered rocks.

The atmosphere seemed crushed between the gloomy weight of the clouds and the dark pall of the sea. I felt as if I were breathing in some new element, an especially thick, cold form of air. There was no wind at all. No ship passed.

Eventually it began snowing. The first flakes were light and drifted slowly, as if they were bubbling softly out of the air, but soon they grew heavier and the real fall began, blanketing the surrounding world. I was wearing gloves, but my fingertips went numb each time I grasped the edge of a rock.

I sat on a high rock and looked out to sea. Each year I came, the weather was different, but the landscape hardly changed at all. On my third visit here the phrase "fixed point observation" had come to mind, and from then on that is what I'd practiced, carefully observing the land and the sea, the opposite shore and the power station. It all seemed to me to be, once again, exactly as it had been. There was the sea, the rocks, the strip of sand, then the cliff beyond and the fields extending inland. I had no idea what was grown in those fields. I once clambered up the cliff, but in March the land was desolate.

The snow grew thicker, filling the air. The chimneys of the power station were no longer visible. The rock was cold now; everything was cold. The entire landscape, everything in the vicinity, had assumed the temperature of the snow. I felt that the only thing still resisting this encroaching world was my own body temperature. I was an alien object in this place. And even my skin, under its protective clothing, was gradually becoming as cold as the snow. Suppose I were to become a part of this rock I was sitting on? Then a day might feel like a second, a whole year no more than an hour.

The skin on my face began to stiffen. I sat with my arms wrapped around my knees and watched the snowflakes being sucked continuously into the sea.

Billions of glass threads extended from the upper air down into the sea, and each flake of snow descended along one of those threads. The bones and joints all over my body had gone rigid and my muscles were chilled; only my inner organs seemed to hold a faint warmth. I wanted to move but forced myself not to. If I were to become a rock I had to remain perfectly still.

As I sat there watching the soundless, endless snowfall, I suddenly realized, with a single flash of insight, that the snow was not falling; rather, the universe itself was full of snow and the world on which I rode was moving up and up into it. Silently, smoothly and precisely, the world sustained this upward motion while I sat on a rock at its very center. The rock rose, and the sea, and that tremendous weight of water, the huge expanse of it, all went on rising; and the I that watched all this rose too. The snow itself was no more than the gauge and measure of that endless upward movement.

How long this would continue and where it would end, whether it would last just as long as the air was filled with snow and whether even a single snowflake had the power to raise the solid world so silently: these were questions that I, now half turned to stone, couldn't answer. I only knew that the world was still rising, moving upward slowly and relentlessly. The sea, too, was reaching upward, as if it knew that with every inch it rose more snowflakes foundered and dissolved. I watched it all for a long time, quite still, quite motionless.

Sasai phoned.

"I'd like to see you, if that's possible."

"Sure. What about a drink somewhere?"

"Right, let's do that. Always assuming you've still got your wits about you."

"Of course. Why? I'm fine—as always. Absolutely sane. What's the problem, anyway?"

"I have a rather peculiar proposition to make. But even though it might sound strange, I'd like you to listen to it seriously. That's all."

We met at our usual place. Sasai was already there when I arrived. He generally sat at the bar, but that day he'd chosen a small corner table.

I sat down facing him and ordered the usual from the taciturn bartender.

Nobody kept a private bottle at this place. You drank what you ordered and paid for it, so there was none of the normal regulars' chitchat. The bartender only talked about things like the weather.

"Anything interesting happen recently?" Sasai asked.

I told him about my visit to Rain Point, very slowly, as if I were mentally reenacting it. I told him how I'd sat on the rock, watching as the whole world gradually froze around me. He listened in silence.

"When I was small," he said, looking into the distance, "I used to look at the snow falling. I'd press my forehead against the cold windowpane and watch it fall outside. I suppose everybody does. It's nice the way it makes no sound. You can't see very far and there's no noise at all, as if the human race has vanished and nothing is moving and the snow will go on falling for hundreds of years. I like snow better than any other weather."

"Didn't you say once that your favorite weather was just whatever it happened to be at the time?"

"Maybe. If you say I said it, I probably did. I suppose I do like any kind of weather, really. Wind and rain make me happy. When I wake up in the morning I look forward to seeing the sky. Does that sound funny?"

We talked for a while about weather and climate: the various displays the sun put on each day, shining on the earth, the air and the vapor in the atmosphere. And clouds. There were dozens of kinds of clouds. Once you looked at them with real attention they never failed to be interesting.

Eventually I asked: "So, what about this proposition, the one I have to listen to seriously even though it's weird?"

Sasai didn't answer for a while. It wasn't that he was searching for the right words or plucking up the courage to say whatever he had to say; the effect was more like that of a large ship slowly changing course, as his mind swung over from the question of the weather to my sudden query. It simply took time. In fact I was still vaguely brooding on the weather myself when he said:

"I wonder if you would mind giving me a helping hand."

"Sure. What with?" I replied casually.

"It's about something I've never mentioned to you before, so I'd like you just to listen for a while."

I got ready to listen.

"I happen to need some money," he said. "It means that for three months I have to concentrate entirely on money-making. That's what I want you to help me with. I'm not talking about the kind of money you get working at an ordinary job; I'm talking about the kind where you try to make as much and as fast as you can. I've got everything lined up. For personal reasons I need to do it just once. I've actually been needing to for some time, but I've always put it off. Now I can't put it off any longer and I'm aiming to do it all in one go."

I was listening without interrupting, as he'd asked me to, but my curiosity had certainly been aroused. This was an area I knew nothing about, but it sounded as if it could be exciting. The whole thing was doubly intriguing coming from Sasai, since I was quite unable to connect the things he was saying with any aspect of him I'd encountered so far.

"More specifically," he went on, "it means handling stocks. I don't suppose you know anything about the stock market, so don't get the idea that you'd be playing the market or actually gambling with stock. Here's how it would work. Certain transactions would be performed every day, stocks would be bought and sold, and these transactions would generate a certain amount of profit. This would go on for three months. It's not a matter of speculating but of following a specific system."

"I don't have any capital," I said, having no idea how I was supposed to fit into this proposition.

"I know that," said Sasai, amused. "I'll provide the capital and the information to make the system work. All you have to do is make the necessary contacts with the stockbroker every day. For certain reasons I can't use my name in public transactions of this kind, so everything would have to be done in your name."

"All it involves is lending you my name?"

"That's right. And I can promise you unconditionally that no money would be borrowed in your name. In fact in no circumstances would we use any money other than what we started with. That should be enough. If it turns out not to be, then it means the system is no good anyway and we'd quit."

I tried to make sense of this by inwardly repeating the story exactly as he told it, but I still couldn't square the Sasai I knew with this kind of proposal. None of it seemed real.

"I can assure you that I do have the necessary capital," he continued in his slow, quiet voice, as if he were reading my doubts before they even formed and had the answers already worked out in his head. "If you have the capital, adequate information and a logical system, and if you put a time limit on your operations and are prepared to stop when you've made the profit you aimed at, then the stock market is a safe, sure way of making money."

"What exactly am I supposed to do?" I asked.

"The time limit is three months. I want you to stop working at the dyer's for that period, but for that period only. It should be easy enough. The boss seems to like you, and you're only a part-timer, so you're free to stop whenever you like anyway. If you can come up with some reason for not being able to work for three months, they'll probably take you on again."

"That should be all right. I can always say I've got to study for some qualifying exam. Since it's only three months it won't look all that funny when I say I failed it. I've been thinking it's about time I got a different job anyway."

"Well, that's up to you. As far as this work's concerned, you'll have to be with me for those three months. We'll rent some kind of office. Buying and selling stocks over and over takes hours, and you're going to be busy. You're the one who'll be going to the stockbroker's and negotiating over the phone. They mustn't know that a customer like me even exists. I'll be the one behind the scenes, reading the market and deciding what gets bought and what gets sold."

"Have you done this sort of thing before?"

"Well, maybe I have and maybe I haven't. But as far as this operation goes, I've known for a while that I'd be needing to make money during this period, so a year ago I did a dummy run. I computerized the system and made imaginary investments. The results were pretty impressive. And this time I'm not just going to rely on newspapers and the radio. I'll hook up with an information agency that can fax me real-time stock reports."

"Sounds all very professional."

"It is. This is serious work, and for three months I'm going to concentrate on it and nothing else."

"What happens when it's over?"

"I'll never touch anything like it again. I'll do something totally different."

"No matter how much you earn?"

"I don't want you to think I'm in this for profit. I don't want money. I'm not doing it to accumulate anything, just to fill a hole that's already been made."

"I could never have imagined you playing the market."

"Well, I'm not doing it for fun. It happens to be the only way I could think of to get what I need."

I decided not to press him any further. I had enough to occupy me, in any case, simply trying to grasp this new situation.

"There's no need to rent an office, anyway," I told him. "We can use my house."

"Ah yes, you said you lived in a big house."

"It belongs to my aunt and uncle. Three years ago they left me to look after it and went off to Canada, and they don't show any signs of coming back. Sometimes they send a postcard that makes me wonder if we're living on the same planet; it's usually all about the size of the latest trout my uncle's caught. They don't have any children and I'm their nearest relative. The house is built on over a third of an acre and it's got more than twenty rooms."

"And you're living there all on your own?"

"I only use three of the rooms. Their lawyer pays the property taxes, and I can get money for the upkeep of the house if I apply to him for it. All I have to do is live there and walk around the whole place once a week to see that everything's all right. Once a month I give some of the rooms and the hallway a quick cleaning, though even that's enough to knock me out."

"It must be quite a house."

"Anyway, it means there are at least seventeen rooms that aren't being used, so you can take your pick of them for the office. You might as well come and live there yourself. If you choose the room furthest from my part you'll be so far away we'll only be able to communicate by cell phone, so we shouldn't get on each other's nerves."

"I hope you won't be one of those super-strict landlords."

"Oh no. Just six months' rent as key money, another six as damage deposit, and I'll only need three years' rent in advance."

"You're a genuine skinflint," he laughed. "Seriously, though, you'll also get paid for your services as regards the actual stock transactions. We'll have to get that sorted out sometime. Naturally any profit made in stock-trading will be in your name, and that will be subject to tax, but I promise to compensate you for that."

"You certainly seem to have thought of everything," I said.

To tell the truth, the whole thing still seemed very odd to me, but at that period I was in a frame of mind that rather welcomed oddity. There was a fixed distance between myself and my surroundings; no matter what I did, I always observed the world about me from that distance. Sasai himself was just another element in those surroundings. So, whatever happened, I was unlikely to get hurt. Of that I was quite sure.

Three days later Sasai arrived. His way of moving house was entirely original. In the morning he turned up by taxi carrying a personal computer, very carefully packed in a cardboard box, which he left in the large, old-fashioned living room I'd chosen as the office. Immediately after that the telephone company arrived and put in a new phone line complete with fax machine. Sasai told me to find a local newspaper shop that would deliver three national dailies and one financial paper starting the following morning, and I arranged that. I also phoned an office supplies shop and ordered a desk, a chair, a bookcase and a filing cabinet. Then I went to a local store and bought stationery.

Sasai came back that evening, again by taxi, bringing everything else he owned. He only needed one trip, since his worldly possessions included not a single piece of furniture and almost no household appliances. Everything fitted into a large backpack and a couple of medium-sized suitcases. I realized now why he hadn't taken up my offer to help him move. I stared at him in amazement as he stood in the entrance hall of my house with his pack on his back and a suitcase in each hand.

"This is the lot," he said.

"Is that really all you've got?"

"Yes. I don't like things accumulating around me. Once you get used to the idea you find you can do without most of them. Up until last year I didn't have the computer, so I could have done the whole thing in one taxi ride. I've even moved house by train. When all this is over I'll get rid of the computer and go back to traveling light again."

He sounded as if he could hardly wait.

The next day I stopped off at a place that would fax information about the stock market and signed a three-month contract. I paid for this with some cash that Sasai had given me when I left the house. By the time I got back, the office furniture had arrived. Sasai had arranged it neatly so that the room really did look like an office, a rather grand one at that. On the desk was a *Company Directory* and other works of reference, with *The Concise Legal Guide* at the end of the row. The computer was already humming away, as Sasai put in one last day on the simulation he'd been running for the past year.

"Everything's working out very nicely," he said. "At this rate there should be no problems when we use real money."

"When should I go to the stockbroker?"

"I'd like you to wait for about a week while I feed the faxed information and what we get from the newspapers into the system. After that we'll start moving the money about."

"Should I open a new account at the bank?"

"No, there's no need for that. All our transactions with the stockbroker will be in cash. A lot of people do it that way, so no one will think it's suspicious."

It was remarkable what a change just a few days had brought to my life. Of all the people I knew, Sasai had always seemed the most distant, the most aloof, yet suddenly his face had become perfectly real. Indeed, he'd become not only real, but

deeply involved in the practical world. This change was fasci-
nating, but a sense of incongruity still lingered. I had grown
used to the idea of Sasai as someone absorbed in far-off things,
an attitude I felt I shared to some extent, and I wasn't sure how
much I trusted this realistic, hardheaded side of his character.

But there was hardly time to entertain this doubt before
business got under way. Sasai himself had said that he would
get no pleasure out of what was only a chore that had to be done,
and I realized he was desperate to get it over with. It was clearly
work he was good at, but that didn't mean he liked doing it.

In fact it soon became just as clear that he was more than
good at it: his knowledge of the financial world and his ability to
put that knowledge into practice were obviously exceptional. As
for me, I did everything according to his instructions. I went to
the stockbroker's after telephoning first, registered as a customer, filled out a number of forms and completed the first day's
acquisition of stock. Sasai had told me the day before exactly
what to say, what to write on the forms, how to behave as if I
did this kind of thing all the time and how to just hint at the
amount of capital involved. It had been like taking part in a play
rehearsal. I was feeling slightly nervous when I set out to pay
my first visit to the medium-sized stock company we had chosen, but I sat down with a nonchalant enough air when I got
there, told the man what needed to be done, dealt with the
forms efficiently, handed over quite an impressive pile of cash,
smiled cheerfully and left. The whole scene had gone off without a hitch. I went outside and hailed a taxi, and as soon as I got
in and sat down, the sweat started pouring out.

Our system worked smoothly. Sasai sat at his desk from
morning till night, reading reports, analyzing them, recording
them, investigating past events on the computer, working out

the overall market trend, forecasting what would happen and, finally, making decisions. These I then transmitted to the stock-broker, and the transactions I made duly turned out almost exactly as Sasai had predicted. The broker's own suggestions were invariably rejected. The basic idea was to stick to a dozen or so stable items that weren't moving much, avoiding any large ups and downs.

On the whole, the people at the stock company seemed to have got the idea—just as we had hoped they would—that I was merely the front man for some powerful investor with limitless capital stashed away somewhere, and that they themselves were only being used as tools in some undercover transaction. This ensured that our relationship was strictly businesslike: they got their fees, but at the same time they were aware that there was little chance of us falling for any schemes they might dream up, though I did vaguely imply that the sums involved in these transactions might go up a couple of digits sometime in the future. Sasai was a genius at this kind of bluff, although he never once bargained on the telephone himself—actually he never even answered it—but merely conveyed his wishes, word for word, through me. He always got the responses he wanted.

He hardly ever left the house, even though once the infor-mation from the market's afternoon session had been sorted out around six o'clock there was nothing else to be done until the next morning. I was always worn out by the unaccustomed strain, so I used to wander out at night, to drink or go to a film or see a couple of casual girlfriends; but as soon as Sasai had fin-ished his evening meal (which he prepared surprisingly quickly in a corner of the kitchen), he'd trek off down the passage to his room at the far end, shut himself up and make no further sound.

One Saturday evening after this had been going on for about

two weeks, we had dinner together. Sasai announced that the
first stage of the operation seemed to have gone all right; he
could afford to ease up that evening and we could have some
real home cooking. He handed me a shopping list and I went off
to the market five stations down the line, where I bought meat,
fish, shrimps, spices and vegetables. Within an hour of my return he'd prepared a number of dishes, wielding the kitchen
knife with practiced skill and making various subtle adjust-
ments, to the level of the gas here or the amount of seasoning
there. In the end he produced a meal that was neither slickly
professional nor amateurishly messy, but something you might
expect from a good, efficient housewife. The salad and dress-
ing, however, were really quite special. I had been so impressed
by the performance, and was so absorbed in the meal that re-
sulted, that I just ate and said nothing. Sasai sat ramrod straight,
eating slowly and obviously pleased with his efforts.

"You're a pretty good cook," I said, at a natural break in the
proceedings when I stood up to get some coffee.

"My mother was hopeless. Whenever I wanted a decent meal
I always had to cook it myself."

I was hoping he might go on to talk about his mother or
some other aspect of his private life, but he didn't say any more.
We just sat there drinking our coffee and talking about the various things you could do with personal computers; for instance,
there was a new piece of software that allowed you to work out
the orbits of comets.

"Like to come to my room?" he said when we'd finished our
coffee. "I've got some good whiskey."

We walked down the long hallway.

"This really is a big house, isn't it?" he said.

"Before the war there were enough people living here to fill
all the rooms," I told him. "My uncle's father was a member of

parliament and apparently there were any number of young men, plus people on this or that errand from the country, plus various hangers-on, all lolling about in corners."

"Lodgers, in fact."

"You could call them that. So my uncle's family lived upstairs. But then, when his father died of a stroke just after the war ended, he said he'd never had any interest in politics and couldn't see any point in taking over some futile rural constituency, so he didn't run. I suppose he must have been sick to death of all those hangers-on, although that, of course, is what politics is all about. Anyway, to cut a long story short, he had a certain amount of private income, so he decided to dedicate his life to fishing."

"And his family?"

"Family's not quite the word. He has no children, and my aunt, who's the blood relation since she's my father's eldest sister, is as eccentric as he is. She used to go fishing with him every day, sitting on the bank and just sort of looking on. She never fishes herself, just watches. And she can keep it up for days, in the wind and the rain, idly watching someone else fish. They're a weird couple."

"So that's why they've gone to Canada?"

"Yes, he said he wanted to catch really big trout, so he decided to go to Canada. That was three years ago. My aunt just went along as if she were only going around the corner to have a look. As far as I know, neither of them had a word of English. And since then the whole house has been mine."

We reached his room, a large Western-style one with a high ceiling and varnished wooden walls. I was struck by the room's emptiness even though I had anticipated it. The only things in it were the original furnishings (an armchair, a sofa and a chest of drawers), a backpack in one corner, a cardboard box, two suitcases and a neatly folded sleeping bag. He took a bottle of whiskey from the chest of drawers and two glasses, or actually metal cups, like the ones you find in camping kits.

"There's no ice or water, but you don't mind, do you?" Sasai said.

"No, I don't want any. Looks as though you've done some climbing."

"When you only live with what you can carry, it is a bit like being a climber. It makes life nice and simple."

"You don't find it inconvenient?"

"They sell everything you want in shops. Rather than keeping stuff all around you, it's better to look on shops as warehouses where things are stored; you just hand over money instead of a ticket when you want to get them. You only buy cheap clothes that'll last a season then be thrown away. Papers or documents you dispose of as soon as they've served their purpose. You only buy paperbacks and throw them out too, once you've read them. You keep kitchen utensils and dishes down to the absolute minimum. You have no furniture. My one piece of furniture is my sleeping bag. Once you've made up your mind to it, it's not all that hard."

"I can see that it makes moving pretty easy, but do you have to move all that often?"

"Fairly often. Still, I've brought you here to see my one possession that violates the principle of keeping everything down to an absolute minimum. My photographs."

I wasn't quite sure what this implied. Was he going to show me photos from the family album? Sasai as a small child all dressed up for some festive occasion? Sasai at primary school lined up with his classmates and a smugly serious expression on his face? Or seated in the middle of a row at a graduation ceremony? And were there going to be great numbers of them? Was it maybe a collection of pornography?

Sasai said nothing more, but proceeded to take a white sheet out of his backpack and pin it onto the wooden lintel, then produced a slide projector from the cardboard box and plugged it in. After preparing the carousel of slides, he sat behind the projector and switched on.

The first image shown on the screen was a mountain landscape; a not very remarkable green valley, with ridges sharply silhouetted against a blue sky. That was all.

Sasai pressed the remote control and a second image appeared. It seemed to show the same kind of mountain, although it was hard to tell if it was actually the same one or not because the colors were so different. Sasai provided no commentary, simply keeping each picture on the screen for a few seconds then switching to the next. There was a steady succession of mountain shots. Some of them, obviously taken outside Japan, showed steeply rising peaks; some were hardly more than gently rolling hills. The collection was an assortment of pictures taken by different photographers in different places and at all hours of the day, and since there was no consistency in either the quality of the shots or in their reproduction, the whole thing lacked coherence.

"They're just photos of mountains, not particularly high and not particularly famous," said Sasai quietly. "But there's a knack to looking at them. You mustn't think about anything. You mustn't look for any meaning. The form of a mountain has no meaning, it's just a shape, and that's what we're looking at. Not meaning, just shape."

"Did you take them?"

"No. Well, I did take a few, but most of them are from books and magazines. This one's from a newspaper, as you can tell because it's so grainy. The point is not to be selective. I take copies of whatever I see printed anywhere that has a mountain shape. That way the individual mountain vanishes and you're left with the abstract idea of the mountain, its essence."

While he was talking Sasai changed the carousel.

"This one's not just mountains but various bits of terrain in general. Empty your mind, think of nothing, pay no particular attention. Just look. This is what the surface of the earth is like. There are deserts, forests, glaciers—nothing extreme; the sort of average you can expect from a random coming together of particles of matter. The color variations that actually exist are roughly what you'll find here, too."

While I watched I began to experience a sense of motion. These images weren't the size of an ordinary projector screen, let alone a television screen. They covered the whole of one wall and thus seemed startlingly real. Although each picture was held for only a few seconds, the different aspects of the earth's surface that they recorded seemed to merge into one, perpetually shifting and flowing, rising, clashing, collapsing, snowed upon, sprouting forests, a succession of endlessly changing images of the earth that were finally subsumed into a single impression.

I gradually found myself being absorbed into this illusion as if I were being possessed by the landscape itself, becoming just one of those elements that make up the surface of the earth. The angles from which the photos had been taken changed constantly, so that with each image the observer had a new viewpoint, now high, now low, now way up, looking far down and across to the horizon, then down again and gazing up into the sky, leaping freely from one perspective to another.

"Interesting, isn't it? Because the pictures don't mean anything. A mountain's worth looking at simply because it's a mountain."

Next we looked at pictures of a river. Unlike the ones we'd

already seen, these were a series of photos taken from one fixed point, the camera set pointing downstream in the bow of a small boat descending a river. The narrow gorge gradually widened, the banks lowered and spread out, then we were between embankments, passing under bridges, and finally reaching the thin line of the estuary to face the deeper blue of the glittering sea beyond. The sense of motion was more powerful than it would have been with an actual moving film, and was oddly satisfying.

After the river, Sasai went back to mountains. I was gradually learning how to look at these photos, how to shut off my own consciousness. My existence had been reduced to that of an eye looking at a total landscape.

A door or window must have been left ajar, for a light breeze entered the room and swayed the extended sheet. The scene projected there moved slightly, giving the impression that the background to that scene, the whole of space, the universe itself, had quivered for a moment. The sense of lightness this gave was wonderful, as if the very air had become a floating cloud that drifted with the motion of the wind.

After going through the set of general terrain pictures once more, we had another look at the river. By now my mind had become accustomed to all the aspects of the world represented in these sets of three dozen slides—to the way it was arranged, its order, simply how it felt. It was like traveling along a road that became more familiar each time one took it.

"Shall we call it a day?" said Sasai, as he pressed the remote control and returned the last slide to its container. The screen became a dazzling square of white, slightly tinged with yellow. Then the projector was switched off and the room went dark.

For a few minutes I said nothing. Sasai got up and turned on a small table light, and we sat in the semidarkness in silence for a while, drinking whiskey. A breeze wandered in again and ruffled the screen, which now reflected nothing.

"I liked your story the other day about the snow," said Sasai. His low, rich voice sounded mature, even old. Since I'd left the dye works and started working at home as his go-between with the stock company, he had begun to seem much older than me. It was true that I'd never quite been able to work out his age before, sometimes considering him as a contemporary and sometimes a good bit older, but now that I was seeing him at close quarters, handling considerable sums of money in a highly efficient way according to some elaborate plan, I found it impossible to think of us as belonging to the same generation.

"The other day I was looking at some photos of terrain similar to what we've just seen, and I got the feeling that the whole surface of the earth had been formed by things falling on it. Of course, geologically, the idea's complete nonsense. Still, I had the impression that I was looking at the original landscape of the earth, when there was no one around, certainly no human beings, to see it. I felt as though I were looking at the matter that formed the mountains, falling and gradually piling up, and the matter that formed the tropical rain forests, a beautifully clear green color, something full of chlorophyll, I suppose, falling softly in the same way, and that that was how the surface of the earth was made."

"Well, the oceans were certainly made by something falling, and that was just as certainly rainwater," I said.

"Yes, but the very first rain that fell and formed the seas was a tremendous downpour. The atmosphere cooled down, and when atmospheric pressure allowed the temperature to fall below boiling point, all the steam in the atmosphere turned into liquid and a fantastic precipitation began, a scalding rain that went on for millions of years. That rain carved away at the rock, melting all the elements that were water-soluble, and they flowed down into the low places on the earth's surface and accumulated there. I don't think we'd adapt very easily to that kind of rain, burning hot, pelting down without stopping onto the dark, dark surface of the earth and raising great billowing clouds of steam."

"The earth was dark?"

"Had to be. Just like Venus is now, with its entire sky covered in thick clouds. Almost no light from the sun would have got through to the surface. It was completely dark."

"So?"

"So I wasn't talking about anything falling like that, but a much gentler, quieter process, with the elements that formed the trees and fields and plains falling just like snow and shaping the landscape of the earth that we know now. I imagined that quiet falling."

Sasai was silent for a while as he went on drinking.

"Whenever I get an image fixed in my mind, I find I can't shake myself free of it for a time. I have this image of that stuff falling and coming together and piling up, and for a while it drives everything else away and just stays there."

"Does that bother you?"

"No, it doesn't. It's just like the slides we've been looking at. You get a different picture of the world in your head, perhaps a picture of a different world. But that's no reason to feel bothered."

Once a week I made my way to the stock company, received a statement of the past week's transactions, gave instructions about new purchases and handed over the money to make them. Every time I left the house Sasai would slip me a small bag containing a considerable sum in cash. The first time he did this I was shocked by the amount, but before long I was used to it, treating the wads in their half wrappers not as money but as a sort of tool, a gadget.

Sasai himself had hardly taken a step outside the house since he arrived. He did go out for a quiet stroll late at night, but he never went very far or dropped in anywhere for a drink; he would just do one quick circuit of the house and come back. He must have decided that, for the three months of this project, nothing should be allowed to break his rhythm as he wrestled with his numbers.

One day on my way back from the stockbroker's I bought three expensive, heavy books of photographs. Naturally this was done at Sasai's request. All three were collections of telescopic photos of the sun, planets, comets and distant nebulae.

That evening Sasai ripped the binding off the three books and pulled the pages out one by one, taking slide photos of them with a camera mounted on a slender tripod and pointing downward. He'd obviously done this sort of thing before, judging by the speed with which he did it and the pleasure he took in it.

"You'd be better off buying a telescope and taking your own photos of the moon or whatever," I said.

"Well, that would be fun to do, I'm sure. But it would be going a bit too far. The bigger the telescope the better, naturally, and you'd want to use it in a place where the visibility was good, so you'd have to build a house in the country somewhere, and the whole thing would get completely out of hand. Eventually your hobby would become just like another job."

"So what you're doing is about right?"

"Yes, just about right. The pictures in the books are a bit too small. But if you make slides of them and blow them up on a screen you feel as if you're looking out of a big window on a spaceship."

The next day was Saturday and the stock exchange was closed. I went off to a film-processing lab in downtown Tokyo to see if I could get the shots Sasai had taken of his three books developed. Told it would take a couple of hours, I decided to visit a large shrine nearby. Two hours is an awkward length of time; there's not much you can do with it.

The ground inside the shrine precincts was firmly trodden down and the stones leading from the entrance gate to the main building had been worn away by so many feet over the years they were actually hollowed out in the middle. I sat on a bench that had been placed unobtrusively in a corner. There was no one else about.

Mulling over recent events, I realized that there were many aspects of what Sasai was doing that I still didn't understand. How had he been able to raise all that cash he was using as capital? It probably wasn't his own money; but if he were using someone else's, surely they could be expected to get in touch with him occasionally. Yet as far as I knew, nobody had even once phoned him or sent him a letter. And since he didn't leave the house, he certainly wasn't meeting anyone.

I knew there was such a thing as undeclared or invisible money and that if it was handled properly it could have more influence in the business world than money that was there for all to see. But Sasai seemed to be far too much his own man to be involved with anything like that.

Again, if our current project really did end up making the kind of profit he said it would, then he must be genuinely clever at it. In that case, it was surprising that he hadn't been entrusted with a lot more money by a lot more people. Why was he doing this on his own?

I'd done all sorts of jobs in my life, but this one was turning out to be by far the strangest. Without even knowing who was really doing it and why, all I could say was that I trusted Sasai; or rather, I just did as I was told, without questioning him in detail about our actual aims.

Pigeons were wandering about on the ground in front of me. It was late afternoon and I was still the only person in the shrine or its surroundings. The birds pecked at anything that looked remotely edible; there must have been a couple of dozen of them methodically investigating the whole area. There seemed no point in thinking any more about Sasai, so I concentrated on the pigeons. After I had watched them for a while, it struck me how limited their existence was. Their manner of walking, their zigzag progress from here to there, the simple repetitive pattern of their evasive actions on meeting an obstacle, all indicated a very primitive level of programming. The way they would spot potential food, approach it and finally pounce on it was pure routine. So was the way they fluttered from one place to another in response to the most elementary impulses—maybe they'd eaten enough, or they despaired of ever finding a crumb in that godforsaken spot, or they'd simply sensed danger. Even their flight was programmed: just plain homing. As long as they stuck to those basic precepts, imprinted on the surface of their brain, they could feed themselves every day.

Yet behind this behavior lay tens of millions of years of pigeon experience. Everything that had happened to the species throughout that vast tract of time was there, recorded in the actual cells of the pigeon brain. The birds I was watching were merely the representatives of some eternal pigeon that had been flying on and on through space and time since the dawn of that unimaginably long period. The familiar gray outline of the pigeon was no more than a transparent window into a time machine, and at the very end of the long corridor of time, incredibly far off, shone the blue sky of the Jurassic Age. As I watched the pigeons mechanically moving here and there, I felt a sudden, intense sense of empathy with their world.

The fact that I was here, now, in this place, that I was a man, alive and linked with other living human beings, meant nothing. It was only a faint pattern traced on the surface of my mind. What mattered was what lay deep, the solid base, the unshakable, time-transcending continuity of being that reduced individuality to the common substance. The important thing was to enter into this permanent aspect of the self. At that moment I was able to see with great clarity, as if from thousands of light years away, myself sitting there watching the pigeons. You could call it a bird's-eye view of oneself.

A tiny old lady in kimono appeared, dragging each leg slightly as she followed the stone path to the front of the shrine, where she ceremoniously joined her hands in prayer. The sunlight made countless circular patterns on the ground as it filtered through the trees, shining indifferently and at random on the pigeons.

Although the next day was Sunday, I was woken early in the morning by the phone ringing. It was a girlfriend who said she wanted to go and see some cherry blossom. As I listened, half awake, to her crisp chatter, I tried to shake the sleep out of my head. It soon became apparent that everything was settled: I was to drive her in my car to a village a couple of hours away to see the blossom there.

"Are you absolutely sure you want to do this?" I asked feebly.

"Of course I am," she said.

So I resigned myself to it, got up, washed my face and put on my clothes.

When I arrived in my car at the designated meeting place, I found she'd brought three other girls with her. Since it wouldn't have been all that entertaining with just the two of us, I didn't really mind; at the same time, I wasn't very happy about being conned into the expedition without having heard a word about three other people coming along. I felt I was simply being used for the easy ride I could provide. Still, the girls were in high spirits, and during the hour's drive on the expressway and the further hour to the village, my small car was at least filled pleasantly with the cheerful sound of their voices and the sweet scent of their bodies.

"The truth is I really hate cherry blossom. It looks so stagy and pretentious," I said at some point during the drive, but nobody took any notice.

In any case, to be quite honest, the trees in blossom didn't look that bad. The village itself was no more than a cluster of fields in the middle of a plain stretching endlessly to the horizon, with nothing to recommend it but a number of cherry trees on the bank of a river running alongside the main road. The buds were still only half open, and the girls all exclaimed about how we'd come too early and how disappointed they were. But I liked it that way. I liked the frailty of the almost pure white flowers and the way they didn't seem to be pushing themselves forward to be admired. I was glad we'd come so far to see them. It was certainly better than if they'd been in full bloom.

"The whole thing reminds me of the kabuki, like the background to some tearjerker about the loyal behavior of an honest fox," I said slyly, but again nobody seemed to be listening.

The girls enjoyed themselves running around the trees, dabbling their feet in the river and eating the impressive variety of snacks they'd brought with them, while keeping a definite distance from me. Even the girl who had called me that morning said no more to me than the other three did, so I ignored them, lying on the riverbank and looking up at the blossom as I thought about Sasai's project.

After a while one of the girls mentioned that there happened to be a fish restaurant nearby, just fifteen minutes away by car. It turned out that this expedition had been her idea. I merely listened and went along. At the restaurant we ate some trout, salt-broiled or boiled with noodles, and cakes for dessert. Although it was early on a Sunday afternoon, we were the only customers.

We left toward evening. When we arrived in Tokyo I dropped the girls off in front of a subway station. Now that the car was empty I opened the window all the way to let in some fresh air. The car itself seemed to breathe a long sigh of relief, and I sympathized with it.

Later, after we'd looked at some slides of the night sky and were drinking whiskey, I gave Sasai an account of my awful day. He seemed amused.

"Not too bad a way to spend a Sunday, surely?"

"I'd have been better off asleep."

"It's a fine thing to be enfolded in the fond attentions of the opposite sex."

"Pity I didn't invite you along."

"There wouldn't have been room for me in the car."

"You could at least have done some of the driving."

"I don't drive. I haven't got a driver's license."

"That's rare these days," I said, and what I'd been feeling and thinking about Sasai for some days now suddenly came back to me. I decided it would be better to come right out with my doubts, rather than hold them back any longer.

"There's something I've been wanting to ask you," I said.

"What's that?"

"I was wondering who we're doing the stock market stuff for."

"Who for? Well, me, I suppose," Sasai said, not looking at all put out by the question.

"So you do care about money?"

"I'm not quite sure how to answer that. But in this case, yes, the money is very important to me."

It was hardly what you could call a clear reply, but I wasn't sure how far to press him. I certainly didn't intend to hinder his work in any way or to stop helping him while we were in the middle of it. I just wanted to know; I wanted to know why a man with no worldly possessions and no settled job, someone who had virtually turned his back on human society to occupy himself with stars and mountains, should have any need for money, and what he planned to do with it.

"Are you going into business or something?" I asked.

"You really want to know? All right, I'll tell you. I've been keeping quiet, not because I didn't think you could be trusted or anything like that, but because I thought it would simply be easier if you didn't know. Still, if you must ..."

"No, listen, you don't have to say anything you don't want to," I said, feeling I'd now put myself in an awkward position.

"Maybe it's time anyway," said Sasai, standing up and switching on the old-fashioned, chandelier-style light, then sitting down and picking up his metal cup of whiskey again. I said nothing.

"I am, as they say, a criminal," he said flatly. "Guilty of the misappropriation of public funds."

I wondered later just how much effort it had cost him to actually say those words, although my response at the time was much simpler, more like assent than shock or surprise, even a feeling of relief, perhaps, that it hadn't been something much worse. I'm still not quite sure why I felt all my doubts had dissolved at that moment.

"Alone?" I asked,

"What?"

"Were you working with someone else, with some organization?"

"Ah, that's what you mean by 'alone.' Yes, I was alone—alone in every sense of the word."

"When we first started this project I thought there might be other people, or some organization somewhere, connected with it. But it certainly never felt that way, I don't know why."

"Alone," he repeated.

"I'm glad," I said.

"Why?"

"If it's just you, I feel I can understand what's going on, so maybe I can help. But where did the capital come from?"

"That's the money I stole. I'm using it as capital so that I can give it all back, the original sum plus the interest that would have accumulated."

"If you give it back, will that make everything all right?"

"It should. As a civil offense, anyway. And in two days' time it will stop being a criminal offense too. The statute of limitations will have elapsed."

"Which means you'll be completely free again?"

"Exactly."

"How long is the statute of limitations?"

"Five years."

"So you've had to spend five years on the run? That must have been awful," I said, as though he were someone who'd had a really serious accident.

"No, it wasn't that bad. Not as bad as I'd expected, anyway. Would you like to hear the whole story?" he asked, lifting his cup of whiskey to his lips. "I used to work in administration at a leading machine manufacturer's. At first it was straightforward administrative stuff, but then, due to one of those freaks of fortune that sometimes happen, business went ridiculously well and the company had money to play with. They decided not to invest it in new equipment or in expanding the business, but to use it as venture capital instead. A few of us were involved at first, but I was the only one who was any good at it. In fact, the others were pretty hopeless. Finally the company put me in charge of investments and just let me get on with it by myself. And things went very well. In a year I made billions for them."

"So you have had previous experience?"

"You could certainly say that. Still, I got bored with it eventually and decided, well, just to push off. This is the part that's a bit hard to explain. For one thing, I can't really describe why I started to feel like that. But I don't mean I regret what happened. It's true that I spent the next five years on the run, changed my name a few times, lived as simply as I could with hardly any possessions and always had to be ready to move in an hour if I thought I noticed something suspicious around me. But I've never felt that I ruined my life because of some rash impulse five years ago or that it's made me miserable. It's almost as if those sorts of judgments could only apply to a different version of myself, though I suppose that's a rather irresponsible thing to say."

"What about the name Sasai?"

"It's not my real name, of course. I saw it written on a door in some country town whose name I can't remember. I've borrowed that man's name once or twice when I needed a residence certificate. In fact I've borrowed lots of names. I'm at the

point where I'd probably think I was being addressed as someone else if you called me by my real name."

It was an odd sensation hearing someone disclaim his name
in your presence. Here was a person I'd known as Sasai and who
responded to that name; it was an accepted part of our relationship. And yet now it had ceased to be attached to him, floating
away into midair and leaving him curiously transparent, as if
he'd lost some kind of covering. He apparently sensed what was
going through my mind.

"I could tell you my real name right here and now, since I
know perfectly well you're not going to run off to the police and
tell them you're harboring a criminal who's about to sneak past
the statute of limitations. And you probably feel you could trust
me more if you knew my name. But as far as I'm concerned,
names don't mean anything. That's one area where I've really
changed over the past five years."

"You were Sasai when I first met you and it's all right by me
if it stays that way."

"It was interesting managing stocks," he went on. "I was handling much larger sums of money than we are now, and splash-
ing it about much more, too. Nothing like the careful system
we're following. The thing was to be able to feel when there was
about to be a flux in prices, to let yourself float with the waves
and just learn to recognize when a really big one was cresting. It
was exciting. There was a constant thrill because of the amounts
of money involved. Then there was the sense of achievement
when your intuition turned out right." He stopped talking at
this point.

"I can well imagine," I put in.

"But I got bored with it," he started again. "You can't do
something like that for long without burning out. But although
I'd had enough, the company wasn't prepared to take me off

the job because I was making these huge profits for them. I didn't have the nerve to lose money on purpose, so the days of nervous tension and weird highs went on. It was like being on stage—a life based on conventions that have nothing to do with the world outside and yet everyone's pretending to believe in them. That's what sustains all the drama and excitement, but it's unreal, so you get tired of it."

"You got tired; and then what?"

"I walked out of the theater. I wanted a breath of fresh air. I felt the best way to get dropped from the cast, from the whole show in fact, would be to run off with some money. At that time our employees could choose either to have their salaries paid straight into the bank or to get them in an envelope, so every month around a hundred of them got paid in cash. When all that money had been made ready one month I got hold of it, walked out of the office and never went back."

"What about your family?"

"I don't really have any. I wouldn't mind having an eccentric uncle, though," he said, and laughed. "The only job reference I ever had was a pro forma note I got from my class teacher at high school. I couldn't see how what I'd done was going to bother anyone like that. I also assumed the company would play the affair down. After all, the money I took was only a fraction of the sums I'd been making for them. They were hardly likely to make a big deal out of it, certainly not to the extent of demanding compensation from a man who'd written a few meaningless phrases about me. I had that all worked out before I did it. I also thought it was quite likely they wouldn't even inform the police, but there I was wrong. An eight-figure sum must have made a hole they thought they couldn't ignore."

"And the statute of limitations for something like that is five years?"

"That's right. My first priority was to get away and then, after I'd settled down a bit, I thought about what I should do. I could either give myself up, return the money and take a suspended sentence, or I could stay on the run for five years. I chose to stay on the run."

He spoke as if he were talking about something that had happened to someone else. Maybe a man's personality does change a lot in five years.

"That's why I think if I return the money with a certain amount of interest the company won't make any further fuss about it. At the time they must have thought they'd never see a penny of it again. Probably forgotten all about it, anyway. After all, it was five years ago."

I muttered a word of agreement but had nothing else to say.

"This is the first time I've told anyone about it."

"Didn't you have anyone who might have helped you? Some woman or somebody ..."

"I didn't try to get in touch with anyone. It wasn't that there was nobody I could trust; I just sort of kept clear of people I knew. I'd entered a totally different world from that of anyone I'd known up to then. Also, if it had occurred to me that I'd need anyone's help doing a thing like that, I would never have done it."

"A different world?"

"Yes. Because I became invisible. I stopped functioning as a link in the whole social network and I also stopped being paid as such. As far as society was concerned, apart from the few anonymous part-time jobs I did, I simply didn't exist. I was invisible."

"Did you spend the money?"

"No, that's the funny part. I didn't. None of it. I always used to laugh when I read articles in the paper about people who'd been caught embezzling the firm's money. They were all the same. They all spent the money as if they had to beat the clock, and by the time they were caught they were almost penniless. It was as if they were playing a game where the first to lose it all and get arrested is the winner. That's why you see them throwing it about in bars and places like that."

"Why do they do that?"

"I don't really know. Maybe because they realize how contaminating it is and feel this compulsion to get rid of it as fast as possible. They stole it in the first place to get some sort of freedom and they end up discovering that freedom is exactly what they don't have. The money becomes a burden. It's like two runaway lovers regretting what they've done the very next morning. Still, to be quite honest, I just don't know."

"But you didn't spend yours?"

"No. Not a penny. That pile of bank notes was my license to be invisible, I thought; like a passport, valid for five years. When the passport expired, I'd return it. Admittedly, I can't claim to have thought of it in exactly those terms when I took the money. In fact, at first I did intend to spend it. I didn't change my mind because I lost my nerve or developed any moral qualms, either. I just gradually realized that it actually was a passport and that I could move about more freely if I hung on to it. So three days after I left the company, in a room in a cheap commercial hotel in some town or other, I made up my mind not to use any of it."

"What did you live on?"

"I'd cashed in all the savings I had in the bank. Then I took occasional jobs at places like the dye works."

"Always in Tokyo?"

"Yes. I tried the provinces, but it's hard to be invisible there. People are too nosy—you can't settle down—so I soon came back. Where it's easiest to feel safe is somewhere like this, an old part of Tokyo with plenty of private houses and apartment buildings. Anyway, I haven't lived all that badly over the past five years." He gave a brief laugh.

The next day was a routine one. At least it seemed to be perfectly routine for Sasai, who did his usual scrutiny of the market, separating the bulls from the bears, recording a reasonable profit and forming his predictions for the coming week. But in my case, it wasn't a normal day at all. After hearing his story the night before, I felt as if I had stepped into his shoes, playing his part more seriously, in fact, than he was himself.

Seen through the eyes of a fugitive, the world becomes a very different place. Most of the things an ordinary person sees and hears every day can be allowed to pass, but with a fugitive nothing can be ignored; everything has to be checked, quickly and casually perhaps, but checked all the same. I found I was noticing even the smallest things: the sound of footsteps going past the house or the fact that the garbage collectors were running a bit late. I tried to stop myself and to behave as I usually would, but acting naturally had become unnaturally difficult. I was caught between two forms of behavior, and wrung out in the process. It was three days before I could adjust enough to put on a reasonably calm appearance.

"There's no need to brace yourself every time the phone rings," Sasai laughed. "You'd make anyone suspicious."

"I know."

"The key thing is being inconspicuous, not cautious. If you're on edge you're bound to stand out. So you try to behave normally, to go with the flow."

"I know," I said again, although it seemed unlikely I personally would ever have much use for the art of being a fugitive.

"In the beginning," he said, "I often used to think it was like the way a grazing animal lives: it doesn't settle down, it just moves on after eating whatever is around it. I was the same. Ranging farther afield was too dangerous. I did everything I could to blend in with my surroundings. I didn't make any sudden movements that might attract attention. I strictly avoided any situation that might bring me into contact with a carnivore. I was a herbivore who'd strayed away from the herd."

I imagined an endless savannah covered with tall, withered grass and, in the middle distance, a single gazelle, barely visible against the purple shadow of the far-off mountains.

"Your five years is like a marathon and I'm just joining you for the final mile."

"That's fine by me. It's nice to have some decent company over the last stage."

The days that followed did feel like a marathon, but one in which there were no other competitors and our man ran on his own. He had entered the final stretch, but he had plenty of strength left and was keeping up a steady pace. We had everything under control. The only worry was that there might be some sudden physical problem—a pulled calf muscle or a stomach cramp—or that some bystander might take it into his head to obstruct him for some reason. So we still held our breath as each hundred yards slipped by, bringing him that much closer to his goal.

Nothing out of the ordinary did happen, in fact. I dealt with the stockbroker in much the same way as I had before hearing Sasai's story. As our profits climbed steadily toward the target we'd set, Sasai switched to a sequence of solid, sure-bet selling; then in the final two weeks, he concentrated on selling all our remaining stocks at a profit. The weather remained depressingly wet.

When we had only three days to go, I think I may have started to feel a certain tension, but Sasai seemed no different at all.
With just one day left, it was the same. Instructions were given
to the stockbroker for the final transactions, information was
fed meticulously into the computer as if we were going to continue with this work for quite a few more days, or even weeks or
months, and Sasai went off to his room looking exactly as he
usually did. He didn't suggest we celebrate the eve of the great
day by having a drink together. As for me, I took a little extra
care making sure the house was carefully shuttered and locked.

Afterward, in bed, I remembered a story about this house
having a secret exit. It had been built by my great-uncle, or so
they said, during the troubles before the war when a quick
escape route might have come in handy. When my uncle first
asked me to look after the house I questioned him about the
secret passage, but he didn't give me any specific information.
I can remember him shaking his head and wondering aloud
which room it started from, either because he really had forgotten or because he just didn't want to tell me.

I was sorry I didn't know. In an emergency, it would have
been wonderful to help Sasai get clear of the house. But I realized almost at once what a ridiculous scenario this entailed.
The idea that a product of the inflated persecution complex of
some ancient member of parliament would ultimately be used
by the friend of the son of the brother of the bride of the man's
own son was so convoluted that even I could see it was funny. I
imagined two or three shifty-eyed characters with a warrant for
Sasai's arrest pounding on the door while I, flashlight in hand,
hastily shepherded him through the concealed entrance in a
cupboard and down into the hidden passage. It was a scene
straight out of a late Victorian adventure story.

The next morning also began as usual. It was a cloudy day in spring, the weather subdued, the kind of day you'd have to make a note of if you wanted to remember anything about it.

"So, you're a free man again," I said to Sasai.

"It looks like it."

"Do you feel free?"

"Not really. Hardly feel anything. In fact, this morning I had the peculiar notion that maybe the police haven't been after me at all these past five years, that I've been running from shadows. Maybe if I'd decided to give myself up yesterday, for example, and gone to the police station, they would have looked through their records and found nobody on them with my name and just sent me home."

"Do you think that's possible?"

"No. It couldn't be. It's just a fantasy. Although it is true that I've been running away all this time from people I've never seen. That's why it suddenly occurred to me that maybe I've never seen them because they were never really there."

I had no idea how I ought to reply to that, so I said:

"Now you'll be able to get a real job, even a passport and a driver's license. It should make quite a difference."

"No it won't. Becoming free isn't going to change my life much. It's true I won't have to put up with a lot of the restraints I've had these last five years, but things will basically be the same. I've got much too used to wandering from place to place when I feel like it and owning almost nothing to start changing now."

"What's the one thing you really want to do?"

"I'm not sure there is anything."

"See those mountains and rivers and deserts with your own eyes, maybe?"

"That's not a bad idea."

"Anyway, today is something to celebrate."

"Yes, it's a special day."

"Like New Year."

"Like any day in the calendar, actually, more or less. The fact is there are no real expiry dates in this world. Nothing is ever completely over, just half done with. It's like the half-life that physicists talk about. The half-life of cobalt 60 is around five years, you know."

I had never imagined anyway that Sasai would start whooping and jumping for joy when his five years were up. The whole time he'd been on the run he must have been as tense as a trip-wire, but now that he was free of that tension the only emotion he felt seemed closer to irritation than relief.

I left the house before noon, went to the bank and opened a new account. I'd been told to tidy up our affairs with the stock-broker and have all the money deposited in this newly opened account. I informed the people at the stock company that we were finished with this particular series of transactions, but hinted that there might be even larger sums involved in some future dealing. Nobody said anything. Once that was done, there was nothing else for me to do.

"What are you going to do now?" I asked Sasai when I got home.

"Haven't thought about it," he replied. "I'll get a lawyer to repay the money to my old company. There's one I used to know, and I'll ask him."

"What about work?"

"I won't do any for a bit, just strap on my backpack and live out of that."

"You're leaving here?"

"Yes. I've stayed here much longer than I normally stay any-where. I feel like going off somewhere. I want to move about. Then I'll start trying to think things through."

Three days later he did indeed strap on his backpack and leave, without any more ado. I didn't see him off at the station but said goodbye at the door. I then went back to my room, sat down and drank some coffee. My head was empty. I had no idea what I ought to do next myself. For the time being, I thought I would probably spend a few days just lazing around.

Everything Sasai hadn't been able to get into his backpack he'd left with me. What I now had was a written record of the last three months, the quite large amount of money I'd earned in that time, a personal computer complete with investment-guide software, and a slide projector with a pile of pictures of mountains, rivers and stars.

I didn't feel much like playing the market, but for the next two weeks or so I did look at the slides a number of times, not during the day, only at night. I would get the projector and the whiskey ready, put up the sheet, then look, over and over again, at the glitter of nebulae five billion light years away. At these times I would feel that Sasai was somehow present, that it was his hand, not mine, holding the remote control. Yet I knew this was an illusion, that I was alone in the room and that if I said aloud anything that occurred to me as I watched the nebulae, coniferous forests, mountain torrents and snowy ravines projected onto that sheet, then it wouldn't be the real Sasai who answered. My mental image of him had rapidly grown abstract, becoming something one could hardly even call human. It was a transformation I welcomed.

*

"I enjoyed those three months," I said, watching pictures of various glaciers succeed each other on the wall.

"I'm glad," said Sasai's voice. "So did I."

"It was like being in high orbit and looking down on the two of us."

"It's not hard to put a part of your mind into orbit. Anyone can do it."

"No, not quite. You're a special sort of person. You have two personalities, for a start."

"You mean I have a split personality?" his voice inquired.

"No. Not split. With a split personality, the two parts clash and confusion results. In your case the two personalities are quite separate, quite independent of each other."

"You mean I'm two different people."

"That's not the way it feels. It's not a question of back and front, either. More like the two sides of the brain."

"How are they different?"

"They're completely different. One is the life-sized you, the one that's happy for today to be just the same as yesterday. The one that's not fazed by being a fugitive. The animal that knows how to read its surroundings accurately, in real time. The lone animal grazing apart from the herd."

"And the other one?"

"The other one is the cosmic version, the one that's sensitive to the passage of neutrinos, the rarefied existence that you find in the dimension inhabited by the mountains, the massifs, the planets, the nebulae. The one high up in orbit. And yet I wonder: why are you two people?"

Sasai simply gave a self-conscious laugh.

"Do you really belong to the same planet as the rest of us?"

"What do you mean by that?"

"I mean that perhaps you've come from a different world."

"That's hardly likely."

"Look at those stocks, for example. Maybe you were using a time machine to read tomorrow's papers every day. In that case, no wonder it was so easy to make a profit and no wonder you found it so boring."

"You're suggesting I've been sent from some other star?"

"That's right. From a star in Ursa Major."

"What for?"

"For no reason, really. You just wanted to see what was going on here at this period in time. So you got a leave of absence and took up residence here for a while. For five years. Now it's over and it's time to go back, so you're leaving."

"But I'm as human as you are. I'm part of the earth, of the surface of the earth. Up until just a short while ago, everybody was like me."

"What's your idea of a short while ago?"

"Around ten thousand years ago, when people's minds were linked directly with the stars. When those distant worlds and the immediate reality of the prey they hunted down coexisted equally in men's spiritual lives."

"And now?"

"Now we have neither. All we have are middle distances, nothing near to us and nothing far, just a false, ambiguous reality that's neither one thing nor the other."

"That reality may be false, but it's one we've created to make life easier for us. We've resolutely built an outer world that keeps us safe. And as I said before, people like you are special now, rarities."

"I know that."

He didn't seem prepared to continue this discussion with me. I had no more to say either. Perhaps I'd already said too much.

The sense of his presence in the room gradually faded. It felt not so much as if he'd left the house as that whatever he was had expanded and become diffused and now occupied a much larger space. The air seemed to grow cooler. After a while I felt that he was something far off, some tiny, vague object flickering in the sky. He was much too distant for me to talk to.

I slowly emptied my glass of whiskey. The last slide clicked back into the carousel. On the sheet up on the wall nothing was reflected but a brilliant, yellowish glow.

REVENANT

1

Arabesque.

I make a grid of two-inch squares on a sheet of thick B4 Kent paper. Holding my breath, I draw the lines slowly with the sharp, fine point of a 2H pencil and a ruler. Then I draw two circles with a pair of compasses and a 2H lead, placing the sharp end of the compasses on an intersection. From each intersection I draw two concentric circles, then many more, circle after circle, with great precision, at the desk placed in the light from the window. The large circle and the small one next to it touch. The two arcs gradually approach each other and when I see they've touched they draw away from each other again. That's most important. If the grid of squares has been drawn correctly, then that depressing mess when the two arcs cross and intersect at two different points doesn't occur.

Next, using the same compasses, I divide each circumference into six equal parts and join these points to the center, making 60° angles where they meet. A number of lines and arcs intersect and link up in various places, creating a geometrical design. They all seem to be knitting together. I wonder which parts I should link up next. On my desk there are patterns I can copy. I could look at them and do it, but there's a problem: when I'm connecting two points precisely with my ruler I mustn't take my eyes off the ruler because it extends farther than the line I want to draw. When I start to draw the line, I have be quite sure about where it's going to stop or else I'll go too far and ruin everything. A 2H pencil leaves a groove in the paper, so if I make a mistake I can't erase it.

It usually takes two hours just to draw the pencil outline of a pattern. I start at nine in the morning and by eleven o'clock I've completed my design in pencil on the white paper. Then I have to choose the colors. In this kind of work, color is critical, so I don't immediately start coloring the design I've taken so much trouble over, not on the Kent paper at least. What I invariably do is make copies of the original design on rough pieces of paper and try the colors there first, so I can get a sense of how they harmonize. Taste is important when you're choosing colors; it's not like simply drawing lines. So I try several different combinations and pick the best one.

By now it's close to midday. I go off to have lunch, leaving the actual coloring till the afternoon. The quieter patients and the staff use the clinic's dining room. The few really serious cases seem to take their meals in their own rooms. I wonder if it's true that their doors are locked all the time? The quieter patients seem like perfectly ordinary people to me. They look as if there was no reason to put them in here in the first place. I wonder if that's how I look to them. Still, I'm not going to talk.

The others talk about all sorts of things while they eat their lunch: TV, some newspaper article, their families, things like that. I just eat my food in silence. I have my memo pad ready in case anybody does talk to me, but practically no one tries to these days, though they did at first. Personally, I don't have anything to talk about. I don't watch TV, I don't read the paper, I don't see my family. I keep quiet and eat up all my lunch properly. I eat quickly. Then I hand in the dishes and go back to my room.

Until half past one I do nothing except sit in a chair and look out the window. There are no bars on my window. If, one fine day, I were to walk out the front door saying "Thanks for every-thing," no one would try to stop me. I mean, that's what I would say if I could speak. I look out the window at the trees, at a white building I can see across the fence and at the distant pur-ple mountains beyond. The mountains I can see here are noth-ing at all like the ones around the ruins at Oneiros.

At half past one I start painting the pattern on the Kent paper with my watercolor set. I choose one of the color combi-nations I worked out in the morning and follow that, creating a complicated arabesque design. When I got back to Japan and was put in here, the first thing I remembered was a book I'd bought just before I went away. It was an album of abstract geo-metrical designs worked out over the centuries by Arab crafts-men as they decorated the floors and walls of their buildings. As Muslims, they were forbidden to portray the human face. The patterns that had originally been done in stucco, tile and alfres-co had been reproduced in the album on paper. I had this book sent from my house, got the staff to give me some paper and a set of watercolors and made it my daily routine, every day from first thing in the morning until late in the afternoon, to draw one of those designs. I now have in my desk drawer 155 ara-besques of various shapes and sizes.

At four o'clock the doctor and the matron come to see me. I've been classified as a voluntary patient, so I try to keep things straightforward during these visits. Having said that, I should point out that the doctor's questions hardly vary at all from one day to the next, and neither do my answers. Since I always give the same responses, I suppose I could just as well show him what I wrote down on my memo pad the day before, but some-how I can't do that. When he asks "How are we feeling today?" I write on the pad with my 3B pencil "Very well" or "All right" or

"Quite happy" and show it to him. If he asks "How's your work getting on?" I reply "It's not really work. I'm just passing the time," or something like that. Then I show him two arabesques, the one I finished yesterday and the one I'm working on today. If the doctor's questions were a bit more searching I'd be happy to write much longer answers, but since everything he asks is strictly conventional I reply in the same way. Recently his visits have seemed pretty routine. Maybe he doesn't think I'm really ill. But the fact is that I really can't speak and I want to get better.

There's always a part of me that wants to get out of here, but in the outside world I know I wouldn't have the courage to talk. I'm incapable of direct verbal communication with people. I have to walk about with a memo pad and write down what I want to say.

I always get the design on the Kent paper finished by five or six o'clock. I've only had to carry it over to the next day three times so far. Each time I complete one it looks so beautiful. I'd like to get down on paper the patterns of the desert in northern Afghanistan as I saw it from the helicopter. Instead of using watercolors, perhaps I could get lots of colored stones, tons of them, and make the design by placing the stones one by one on the ground. If one side measured half a mile, I would have an arabesque corresponding to hundreds of square miles of desert. It would take years to complete, working at it every day, spending a lifetime at it. That's the way I'd like to spend my life.

But I could draw thousands of arabesques on paper and still not achieve what I'm aiming at. It doesn't matter how complex and subtle my design is, or what color combinations I come up with, or how careful I am to keep the colors from overlapping, or how well I wash the brush after I'm done, using lots of water to be absolutely sure the colors don't get mixed, or how much effort I make to lay on the colors precisely within the lines drawn by a device with a 2H lead in it: none of it matters because when the design is complete I can never see the face of God in it. Sometimes when I've painted in only a couple of the colors, I seem to glimpse it, but as I fill in the other colors the face gets lost in the pattern as a whole. Maybe I'm going about it the wrong way.

2

I eat my three meals a day as I'm supposed to. And I take them seriously, because food is important. When someone eats, he puts a piece of the outside world inside him. The substance of his own body is gradually altered by this, giving him energy and, therefore, life. What used to be chicken or sardines or broccoli before being eaten is broken down inside his body into tiny particles, which then join up again in a different order, becoming part of himself. Things that are eaten lose their own shape and qualities and merge with the body of the person who eats them.

I didn't produce the kind of report expected of a member of an expedition. Tajil gave a detailed public explanation of the accident before I returned, so everybody knew about that, but in response to all the other questions, to which only I had the answers, I said nothing. I didn't say what the remains at Oneiros were like or why Pierre hadn't come back. I didn't suggest that a second expedition be sent to find Pierre or who should be sent. I didn't indicate whether I'd be prepared to go on such an expedition myself. I made no reply to any such questions. I didn't reply because I couldn't.

The committee that had dispatched the expedition, as well

as the TV network I worked for that had sponsored it, put me through a tough interrogation. But whenever the questioning got too tough I tended to lose consciousness, falling into a deep sleep. It really was a deep sleep—in fact almost a coma, clinically speaking—and not some act I was putting on. The EEG print-outs showed this quite clearly. I would stay asleep for twenty-four hours and there was nothing I could do about it. After this had happened several times, I lost the ability to speak. All I could manage in response to the questions was to write down my answers. I no longer felt like talking to other people or even asking them for anything. If my meals didn't appear, I was prepared to put up with hunger pangs for hours without complaining. When my interrogators noticed the condition I was in, they gave up their attempts to get at the truth and it was decided to put me in here for medical treatment.

As for what happened to us, our thoughts at the time, our relationship with the place whose existence was the root cause of everything that transpired, our final decision: I could talk to Pierre even now about all these things because there are still things to talk about. It would be part of a conversation that could, in a way, be considered unending. But I can't speak to ordinary people. There's nothing to be said to the average inhabitant of this world.

And so, because I can't speak about the one matter of really vital importance to me, I've abandoned speech altogether and opted for silence. Maybe the decision was made somewhere in the deepest levels of my mind not to talk about these things, followed by some breakdown in my mental power source, so that the decision can't be reversed. The result is that I am now undergoing mild treatment in this clinic every day, though in practice it's more just a sort of convalescence. My daily routine consists only of drawing these arabesque designs. The doctor smiles and says it's most important that the cure be gradual, but he doesn't look too confident about the outcome. However, since I like it here and the doctor seems to feel it's another interesting case, we get on pretty well. That's my situation at present.

The doctor thinks I've experienced something that could be described as shock, which accounts for my not being able to speak. His interpretation is that I must have done something I simply can't put into words, or seen the sort of thing the human eye should never look upon, and that's why I've withdrawn so completely into myself. Soon after I got here, I heard him saying as much to some journalists. The doctor has no idea what really happened. There's nothing surprising about that, either.

I wonder if he thinks I might actually have eaten Pierre. In one very special sense of the word, it could be said that Pierre was eaten, but not by me. I haven't absorbed his body into mine, broken it down and reassembled its various elements so that they combine with mine, making him part of myself. If I had done something like that, could it cause—as the doctor seems to think it could—my sudden inability to speak? But I'm not unable to speak; it's simply that I have decided not to speak because I know it's impossible to offer any acceptable explanation of what happened there.

Tiny unicellular algae absorb sunlight and carbon gas and turn them into energy. Then small animal plankton eat the algae, breaking down the carbohydrates, starches, cellulose, chlorophyll and other higher chemical compounds that have been stored inside them and recreating them in new forms. Small fish eat the plankton, then large fish and cuttlefish eat the small fish, then even larger fish, like tuna, eat those fish and the cuttlefish and, finally, I eat them. But nobody eats me.

I am algae. Every living thing is algae. My thoughts are only a repetition of algae's thoughts and the thoughts of small fish and cuttlefish and plankton and tuna at all those different stages, like some massive mental playback. I am algae, small fish, tuna: I contain all of them and have no existence independent of them. I am like a combination of tiles, a multicolored mosaic, a pattern of bright stones in the desert, an enormous arabesque. The act of eating is like the act of assembling stones to create a design.

I did not eat Pierre. To say that Pierre was eaten is not a wholly inappropriate way of putting it, but it wasn't I who ate him.

3

Seen in the context of the whole, an individual life, with all its thoughts, is perhaps a trivial and pointless thing, just one line in the great design, a single pixel among millions. But for the individual concerned, his own existence overrides and outweighs all other created things put together. Change the subject, change the point of view, and the whole structure of the world alters completely. That alteration is so vast it makes one flinch before it.

Has the world been made for me and am I at its center? Or am I something quite inconspicuous, occupying one tiny corner of it? I prefer not to answer. Either view seems feasible to me.

Pierre and I were talking on the riverbank near the site of Oneiros. We had just finished our evening meal of fish caught in the river, some of the gooseberry-like fruit that grew along the bank, and canned vegetables we'd brought with us in the dinghy.

That day Pierre had encountered his own past.

"I met myself as a child today," he said. "It was wonderful, going back that far into the past."

He spoke in a low voice, gazing into the flames of the fire as if searching for the memory of a pleasure that was already growing vague.

"Who did you say you met?"

"Myself when I was small. I was sitting in the open space there and a child walked toward me out of the music. He sat down beside me and we talked for a while. We said nothing of any importance, but we communicated our feelings perfectly. It was very nice. Then the child smiled and asked me if I knew who he was."

"And?"

"I just looked at his face, and he giggled and said, 'I'm you when you were small.'"

"So you met yourself?"

"He said 'We're all here. All those that aren't in your world are here. We don't exist separately from one another; we're all dissolved into nebulae throughout space. I've only appeared in the shape of your younger self to draw you out like this. I'm not confined in this human form forever.' That's what he said, anyway."

"You heard his voice from out of the music?"

"Not just a voice. The child was really there."

"Ah," I said, feeling suddenly sad. I didn't imagine I'd ever meet myself as a boy. I didn't think I was capable of such an experience. I wouldn't be allowed in that far. It was because it was Pierre that the child had appeared. Pierre and I were different. I'm not quite sure how to put this, but it's as if the shell of my ego is too thick.

"He said this was a relay station," Pierre blurted out after a while, his voice resonating like the voice of Oneiros itself.

4

It all started with a single aerial photograph. During the Afghan war, a Soviet reconnaissance plane was hit in the wing by a ground-to-air missile, but just managed to stay aloft. Virtually out of control, it flew over wild and unexplored mountainous terrain until the pilot was able to get it back over Soviet territory. There it crash-landed and the pilot was killed. The plane's camera happened to have been set on automatic, as became clear later, but the authorities who handed the set of photographs over to a team of special analysts probably assumed they had no significance. The film had been exposed over part of the western Karakoram range, a mountainous region where the borders of the Soviet Union, Afghanistan and Pakistan meet, totally uninhabited and uncrossed by any major air routes. An eccentric geographer had passed near the area a few decades earlier, but there was nothing in his report to interest non-specialists.

The photographs were enlarged and analyzed in detail. One of them showed what seemed to be the ruins of a stone fortress, or at least something man-made, though the theory that it might be a natural feature created by a series of freakish accidents couldn't be ruled out. It lay in a valley whose sinuous windings followed those of a narrow river, which was unusually full of water for this region, and looked like a cluster of buildings covering an area of several hundred square yards. The whole complex stood out sharply from its surroundings. Its shape was more or less irregular and the roads (if they were roads) that ran between the buildings formed a peculiarly intricate network.

The general impression was of a small but extremely disorganized town, though even when the photos were blown up as far as they could go it was still impossible to tell whether the whole thing was a natural or an artificial phenomenon.

The site was named the Oneiros ruins after the nearby river. If it represented the authentic remains of some ancient civilization, it was thought that some written record of it might exist. But historians combed through documents relating to the countries in the surrounding region and found nothing conclusive. There was just one thing that was suggestive. An entry in the records of a once-flourishing kingdom to the south stated that during the reign of a certain king a detachment of soldiers was sent to investigate the truth of a tradition that an eternal city of stone could be found along the upper reaches of the Oneiros River. But the entry was so brief it didn't even state whether the soldiers returned or not, or describe what they reported if they did.

This aerial photograph of mysterious ruins attracted worldwide interest, so it wasn't surprising that the idea was soon put forward of sending a team to investigate. The plan was that a small search party should go out first to determine whether or not the remains were genuine, approximately when the complex had been built, and on what sort of scale. When all that had been established, a proper expedition would be mounted. For the quite accidental reason that the television company I worked for happened to be sponsoring the preliminary investigation, I got to be a part of it. I was the only Japanese member of the group; the rest consisted of two Russians, one of whom was the leader, an Indian archaeologist, an Iranian historian and a brilliant young cultural anthropologist from France, Pierre.

The team gathered in Kabul. That was the first time I met Pierre. I found him very reserved for a European, but he didn't make a bad impression on me. He was quiet, never venturing his opinion until asked, and capable of sudden physical activity when it was required. I can remember thinking that I would probably get on well with him.

5

As long as I stay in this clinic I will remain virtually cut off from other people. This means living in just the opposite way to the life embodied by Oneiros, that sustained condition of heightened existence to which ordinary "life" bears almost no resemblance. Is there no other choice, then, than that of either practicing the principle of Oneiros or rejecting it utterly? Is it impossible in ordinary society to make contact with people in a way that even remotely approaches the Oneiros idea?

It probably is impossible. So basic a denial of the concept of individuality leaves no room for compromise. When all becomes one, when the idea of a part or an individual no longer exists, the self must disperse into the whole. But in actual society, where distinctions are retained, to behave according to that principle would be like going naked among people wearing armor. One's skin would be ripped to shreds in an instant.

Because I dread that outcome, I stay in my room and refuse to speak. For all communication, I rely on the written word. If I were to utter even one phrase I would be allowed to leave, but I remain silent.

I once asked Pierre if he thought the site would affect all visitors in the same way. I wondered if it worked automatically, like some kind of machine, sending the same messages to anyone who happened to stand in that open space. Or did it change its methods according to whoever came? If it did react similarly no matter who was there, it could be seen as a kind of trap, the way the Venus's-flytrap catches flies: the insect pops inside and the door automatically shuts. But if the site were a trap, why did it respond in different ways to each of us, to Pierre and me?

It was possible, perhaps, that the people who went there had already been chosen. It's a fact that only two of the six who had originally planned to reach Oneiros actually arrived. Was that purely accidental or was it something the place itself had arranged? I didn't know the answer, nor did I believe I ever would know. I was never sure what role the great eagle played in it all, either. Why should the site, or whatever power lay behind it, linked up somehow across infinite space, go to all this trouble over two men? Why invite creatures who existed as individual organisms to participate in a different order of being? What could have prompted its interest in us? Was it carrying out some kind of selection process? One possible proof of that was that I was now here: I had come back and Pierre hadn't.

Again, can one even begin to talk of a "consciousness" in terms of something so extensive and ineffable? When one small, separate organism affects another, it certainly comes into play, but when existence as a whole is involved …? And were Pierre and I important enough to justify the attentions of such a "consciousness"? Did it see us as potential proselytes? Did it need such proselytes among our kind? If, as Pierre maintained, existence on this planet was controlled by some principle existing above it, did it need to go to so much trouble to let us know? Were we worth it? Was I? I didn't know. I still don't know.

6

The rubber dinghy made smooth progress. The river flowed

gently and the water was deep enough for the outboard motor not to touch the sandy bottom. Occasionally one caught a glimpse of fish darting through the clear water. Since the engine was low-powered, we weren't moving fast, proceeding upstream at about the same rate as the current was flowing against us. As I sat in the stern steering the dinghy, the pleasant vibration of the engine traveled through the tiller to my hand and made me feel drowsy.

It was the day after the accident, the day Pierre and I set out alone for the place, so naturally images of the disaster still haunted us. Both of us also had serious reservations about the decision to continue with the expedition. We said little to each other, deep in our own thoughts about those who had died, and about Tajil, who had stayed behind by himself.

But that night, camped on the riverbank and stretched out beside the fire, we slept surprisingly soundly. Perhaps it was the good kind of fatigue brought on by our river journey that did it. Then the next morning, after we'd set off upstream again in the pleasantly chilly dawn air, we began exchanging occasional remarks. From the beginning, Pierre and I had got on well and, since we were both aware of that, we tended to work and spend time together. At least that's how it appeared to me then, although when I think about it now the first time we really talked seriously to each other was on that trip up the river.

The river ran through a gently undulating plateau. In the distance could be seen the blackish shapes of hills under a purple sky. Maybe they weren't hills but enormous sand dunes. There was nothing green in the landscape, only parched soil and the river slowly flowing through it. Just as slowly we drifted up the river, pushed on by our feeble yet remarkably noisy engine. Along a strip no more than a dozen yards wide on each side of the river, grass and trees drew sustenance from the water, but beyond that there were only the dry, rocky lines of hills stretching away interminably. Not one spot of greenery was visible in all that vast expanse. Much farther off we could see a range of white mountains. Our destination lay quite close to them.

"I wonder where this water comes from," Pierre said from the bow of the dinghy, looking back at me. He almost had to shout to make himself heard above the noise of the outboard motor.

"There must be some large source of water way upstream."

"What kind of source?"

"Melting snow. Something underground. Maybe a glacier."

"It must be huge to supply this amount of water."

"A lake, maybe. That's why the supply's so steady."

"I wonder how he's getting on."

"Tajil? Just sitting there waiting."

"When will help arrive?"

"Things will start moving when they realize the helicopter is overdue. It'll all depend on how soon they can get hold of another one."

"Should we have waited?"

"No. I wanted to get going. We'll never have another chance like this. We won't be able to do a proper survey, of course, but this was only a preliminary expedition anyway. All we have to do is work out if it's the remains of some human construction or a natural rock formation. Then we go back."

"That eagle's circling overhead again," Pierre interrupted.

"Are you sure it's the same eagle?"

"I'm beginning to think it was maybe that bird that caused the accident."

"The eagle?"

"I didn't want to make a big thing of it at the time, but I

thought I saw something like an eagle diving down toward the helicopter, and then it happened."

Now that I thought about it, I could also remember thinking I'd seen something black, high above us, heading straight for the helicopter.

"But how's an eagle going to make a helicopter crash?"

"Exactly. I can't imagine any bird wanting to tangle with something like that."

"Do you think he's following us?"

"A lookout, perhaps?"

But we'd grown tired of looking straight up and soon forgot about it.

We stayed in midstream all day, pulling in to the bank as evening fell. After mooring the boat firmly to a tree, we made camp, just as we'd done the day before, gathering dead branches for a fire, brewing up coffee and making a supper of canned food and boiled potatoes.

The sense that we'd completed another day of our journey gave some satisfaction. The memory of the accident was bad, but at least we hadn't been sitting about feeling sorry for ourselves. Here we were actually doing something. That helped, as did the knowledge that we'd covered more than sixty miles in two days.

"I wonder what the place will look like," I said, not addressing the remark to Pierre in particular so much as thinking aloud.

"A kind of fortress. Or maybe a town. Buildings made of large stones, clustered around narrow streets," Pierre replied automatically, as if he were describing not a place he knew but one he'd read about. "Those streets, which could just be gaps between the rock walls, are very narrow and winding, and there are places where you can't get through. The stones are extremely irregular, so they may not be buildings after all. There are no doors, apparently. There don't seem to be interior spaces. Still, they're buildings for those who know how to use them. And there are a lot of them. What else? There are openings that look like windows, but they're really just holes between the stones, a bit like small wind tunnels."

"How do you know so much about it?"

"I read the relevant literature."

"Come on—there is no relevant literature, certainly nothing that gives that sort of detail. I've read all there is."

"Perhaps there isn't. Still, I don't think I'm confusing the Oneiros site with somewhere else. I'm certain it's just the way I described it."

"Well, we'll know when we get there."

I didn't say any more. We both had an odd feeling about it, but we also seemed to feel it was best to keep such intimations to ourselves. The more we talked, the more distant we'd grown. So we crawled into our sleeping bags and fell asleep by the fire.

On the afternoon of the next day we arrived at the ruins of Oneiros, although we couldn't see them directly from the river. The first thing we came across was the entrance to a V-shaped gorge running due south from a spot near the river to the ruins themselves. No water flowed between the steep, unbroken walls of this narrow defile. We knew the place because its location, shape and direction matched up exactly with the aerial photograph, so we stopped there and continued into the gorge on foot after first dragging the dinghy up onto the bank. We carried light day packs, since even though the site appeared to be only a mile or so from the river we had no idea how long it would take to get there. The only way to find out if it was an easy walk or not was to walk it.

I was excited that we were finally going to see the ruins, but Pierre seemed almost downcast. While we were pulling the dinghy up onto the bank and getting ready to set off for the site, I'd had to encourage him before he would actually do anything. He didn't seem reluctant so much as apprehensive. But I didn't let his obvious lack of enthusiasm bother me, hurrying on ahead in my eagerness to see the ruins with my own eyes.

It took us over an hour to walk that mile or so. The gorge was an ancient riverbed. In the distant past, water must have flowed through it, but it had dried up and grown wild over the centuries; parts of the cliffs had collapsed and the way was strewn with jagged rocks and boulders that made the going difficult. A north wind blew hard at our backs. Since the only source of drinking water was the river, the camp would have to be set up there and this two-way trek would have to be made every day until we'd completed our reconnaissance.

The gorge had been leading due south, but now it turned slightly to the right. From that bend I could see the ruins stretched out before me. The narrow valley widened a little at that point, with the cliffs now towering above it quite perpendicularly and, depending on the angle from which you looked at them, even appearing to overhang it. And there at the far end of the valley, extending from one side to the other and blocking the exit, were rows and rows of stone buildings. It was immediately clear how difficult it would be to pick them out from overhead. That one photograph had been a truly remarkable piece of luck, and it was obvious why repeated analysis of satellite pictures had always failed to confirm what the photo had revealed. There was only a narrow strip of sky overhead and the site could be seen only from a certain angle. Our search for the easiest path through the gorge had brought us to a point halfway up the side of a cliff, so when we first saw the site we were looking slightly down at it.

At that distance, it was still impossible to be sure whether it was a man-made or a natural phenomenon. My immediate reaction was to sit down where I was, flooded with a sense of wonder as I absorbed the entire view; but the expression on Pierre's face was one not of wonder but of fear.

"What's wrong? Does the place give you the creeps?"

"No. I was just thinking that we'd finally made it, that's all."

"But this is what we came for."

"Yes. But I hadn't expected it would have such power."

"What power?"

"I'm not sure. It's just that I feel the place has been controlling us all along, even when we were still far away. It's as if I was drawn here all the way from France, I don't know why. Standing here I can feel it all the more—like a strong wind blowing from that direction."

"The power of darkness?"

"No, not that, just something powerful."

"Come to think of it, you *must* have known about the place already. From here it looks exactly the way you said it would."

"That's another thing I don't understand—where I could have got that knowledge."

"Anyway, let's go and look."

"Yes. We've come all this way, after all. I could hardly turn my back on it and just go home."

It was still hard to tell whether what we were looking at were buildings or rock formations, whether the gaps between them were really pathways or not. Getting closer made it no easier to decide. Since our main task that day was to get a general picture of the whole place, and because it didn't seem especially dangerous, we agreed that if for some reason we lost contact with each other we would meet up in an hour's time at the entrance. We checked our watches and compasses and, with the wind still blowing at our backs, went down into the site.

The passage we used was narrow and winding, sometimes coming to a dead end, sometimes branching off in two or three directions. We went on cautiously, very slowly, watching each step we took and keeping an eye out for landmarks, hardly speaking to each other. The passage floor was pocked with indentations and scarred with peculiar ridges and hollows, making one wonder if it could possibly have been constructed for human beings to walk along. There were step-like formations, but all irregular in height, some as much as three feet high.

Water had obviously eaten away soft areas of the rock, suggesting that the whole site could have been created that way over the centuries. But why had the water stopped flowing through the valley? Again, if water was the active agent, why weren't more of the surfaces rubbed smooth? Only a series of highly unusual natural events could have produced such formations. Then there were these rows of almost square rocks, looking very much as if they'd been lined up next to each other: surely they implied the work of human hands. Not to mention the fact that each rock was roughly the same height, about fifteen feet.

Walking along those passages I had no sense of fear. Pierre also seemed quite composed by now. I wasn't expecting some monster to be lying in wait around the next corner, or a deep pit to open up suddenly before me, swallowing me, or the walls to slowly close in, crushing me. Yet I still had the feeling I'd had from the beginning that there were presences about us, or rather, that the whole place was suffused with the aura of some larger presence. It wasn't that feeling you get when you sense that one or two other people might be near, but an intimation of something drifting, rarefied, diffuse, something at once weightless and transparent. It's impossible to express this in words because whatever it was surrounding me—and Pierre as well, who was walking a few yards behind me—was something beyond description.

And then, when we entered an open space that looked rather like a small town square, the music started.

7

I'd thought the easiest way to give some idea of the mysteriousness of that place would be by starting with the music, but it turns out that that's the hardest thing of all to describe or explain. I'm beginning to think it's impossible to convey a sense of it to someone who hasn't actually heard it.

When we first noticed it, it seemed to have just started. It could, of course, have been going on for some time, our ears having only slowly become attuned. Perhaps that sense we'd already felt of some ineffable presence had been merely this music, faintly heard. Whatever the truth of the matter, both Pierre and I became aware of it at the same moment. He looked at me, raising a finger to signal me to listen, and I immediately understood the meaning of the gesture.

At first I heard only the sound of the wind, but as I listened I realized that countless lesser noises were hidden within that faint, overriding sound. I sat down on one of the small rectangular stones scattered here and there around the open space and Pierre sat on one on the opposite side. The music was like the sound of the wind passing between the stones, but it was too complex and changeable to be merely wind; there were rich harmonics within it, numerous clear sounds combining to suggest a depth more profound than that of any natural harmony.

I was absorbed into the music and held entranced by it, as if I were drinking from some deep well of water so crystal-clear I could see right to the bottom, tasting its depths in one pure drop after another. Gradually I became aware that the music was actually made up of voices and that they were ones I'd heard before, belonging to people I knew. But they weren't just voices from my own vividly remembered past, of people I'd actually met; I could hear ones familiar from records and movies, even people I knew only by name and whose voices I had imagined, people from as far back as a thousand years ago. Not that I could distinguish any of these voices from the others; I simply felt a certainty welling up from deep inside me that these were the voices I was listening to.

Then again, perhaps it wasn't just voices I could hear but musical instruments, too. The more I heard, the more convinced I was of this; they seemed so perfect for that place—for me as well. Yet even the idea of instruments is wrong. These sounds weren't produced mechanically; they were simply the outcome of all the varied sounds existing in the natural world. They weren't made by musicians, yet each one had meaning and they formed a harmony among themselves. All things in existence sang out, and men were moved to sing together with them, all resounding at the very heart and center of the universe, all combining with the perfect harmony that prevailed there. And what reached my ears was the pure essence of that music. I heard it then. I still hear it now.

I was listening to sound itself. No one was required to tune it or to play it. It was the sound of whatever lies at the base of everything that exists, including our own existence, and since it was that most basic of all things, inevitably it could know no discord. All this I realized as I sat there without moving, listening to sounds at once far and clear, faint yet plain: that perfect music.

How long it continued I hardly know. As my body measures time, it seemed to go on for a long while, but as the world works, it was an instant. Since eternity is our standard here, and in eternity even the longest periods are moments, I think it must only have been a moment. In terms of my consciousness of time I was no longer the master of my body or my mind. I was not the one judging such things.

I looked up and noticed that the narrow band of sky above us had darkened, and then glanced at Pierre. He'd noticed the same thing and was just standing up.

We said nothing as we picked our way awkwardly along the stony track back to the riverbank. It didn't occur to either of us to try to discuss what we'd heard. There was no doubt that we had both heard the same thing, that we'd been linked by similar cords to the same source of sound. And no doubt he, like me, was feeling overwhelmed by the mystery of this place we'd found.

So we did everything in silence, there on the bank of the river: unpacked our things, lit a fire, brewed coffee and ate our meal of canned food, potatoes and bread. And the reason we didn't break the silence between us was that it seemed to us we could still hear the music in our heads. We wanted to go on listening and not confuse the music with the sound of our own voices.

In that way our first day at the Oneiros site ended. We laid out our sleeping bags on the bank and slept. With nightfall the wind dropped and the stars shone clear in the sky, a great army of stars brandishing the spears of light, shouting with the voices of light, scattering their light indifferently in all directions.

8

We could see the great eagle almost the whole time now.

Pierre still maintained that the bird had had something to do with the helicopter accident. I didn't know what to believe, but he seemed convinced. People believe what they see; they also think they've seen the things they believe, which is pretty much the same thing. Perhaps Pierre saw deeper into the heart of things than I did. The idea that the site somehow chose the people who were to visit it doesn't seem so unlikely to me now.

For whatever reason, the great eagle circled continuously overhead. He seemed to be watching us, maybe even watching over us. One felt safe with him always there, confident that no mishap, no sudden stumble on the stone steps, would occur while he was there. Yet it also crossed my mind that if we tried to leave he might do something to stop us. But no, I told myself, he'd probably let us go, deciding that he'd misjudged us and that he would be more careful next time.

Just once the eagle did disappear, but not the way a normal bird would. When a bird vanishes from sight, one can usually assume that it has flown off somewhere, to the mountains or over the horizon or into some distant cloud. But this one disappeared while I was lying on my back on the riverbank watching him. He simply went higher and higher into the blue sky, flying up and up until he was absorbed into the firmament. He never seemed to move horizontally; like the sun and the moon, he was already so high up he appeared to be almost directly above our heads. And when he vanished he just flew higher, because the only motion he knew was vertical.

9

How did it happen that Pierre and I were the only ones to see the place? The river indicated clearly enough where it was and the photographs the Russian reconnaissance plane had taken provided map coordinates, so its whereabouts were known almost from the start.

The problem for those before us had been the river. The Oneiros River rises in the Pamir mountains and, after gently traversing a dry plateau that is mostly desert, descends to the plain below as a fierce torrent. Not only is the current particularly strong, but the riverbed is a clutter of rocks, making navigation impossible. This fact alone would explain why the site had remained unvisited, except by that one legendary expedition.

In the case of our own expedition, the whole party was to have been ferried by helicopter from Kabul to a point upstream of the rapids, the plan being to continue by boat across the plateau. The site itself was on the far side of the plateau, where the foothills of the Pamirs start. Since it was impossible to transport the whole party plus all the equipment at one go, it was decided to do it in two shifts. On the first trip the helicopter took three of us: myself, Pierre and the Iranian archaeologist, Tajil, together with all the supplies, such as the rubber dinghy and the various stores and provisions. The remaining three members would come on the second trip with the equipment needed for the survey.

We left Kabul airport at seven in the morning. The 250-mile flight took about two hours, the last half of which was spent following the course of the river. Seen from above, the river flowed along a deep, narrow, meandering valley that had carved its way through high mountains. The mountains themselves looked as if they had been hacked out randomly with a gigantic ax. For this reason it was only possible to glimpse the river occasionally, although it was easy to imagine the ruggedness of the terrain it ran through. The mountains were dark gray, rough and gritty-looking. One got the impression that their shape was sustained by the action of equal and opposite forces, one forcing them up and the other pressing them down. As it flew between the twin expanses of the mountains below and the purple sky above, our helicopter must have looked no bigger than a mosquito.

For the last sixty miles, though, we dropped down into the deep gorge cut by the river, flying perilously between cliffs on both sides. The ground was now more than six thousand feet above sea level and our heavily loaded helicopter couldn't even maintain the altitude of the ridge; the pilot had no choice but to fly down into the gully. So we groaned our way along between those towering walls; and if you could forget for a moment that your own life was being put directly at risk, the view was marvelous. Holding my breath, I looked out through the helicopter's plastic dome at the scarred and broken rock faces, at the plants that had managed to find a foothold on them, at the glittering water far below and at the spot where, as it reflected a white sun, the river shone with a powerful, concentrated dazzle.

Pierre had his face pressed against the opposite window as he too gazed down, absorbed in the landscape. He was as fascinated as I was by this uninhabited world, these cliffs never seen perhaps by human eyes before. The expression on his face was enough to tell me that his mind was working in the same way as mine. We both wanted to dissolve somehow into that barren world. We didn't care about leaving proof of our existence on this earth; we wanted to become part of it, dust floating in its air. We wanted our souls to be scattered among its millions of birds, to participate in their existence. These were our feelings as we gazed at the cliffs, and when occasionally we caught a glimpse of a nest, we couldn't help envying the bird its way of life.

But Tajil wasn't that kind of person. I knew this because I'd worked with him while we were preparing for the expedition back in Kabul; it had been clear at once that his was a healthy, practical approach to life. He had traveled this far from civilization because that was the job he'd been given. He had no fear of this empty world and no desire at all to lose himself in it. While Pierre and I went on staring at it, Tajil slept soundly on his hard seat, oblivious even to the racket of the engine and the occasional buffeting by pockets of air.

When we had traveled far up the valley, the pilot gestured downward. Looking, I saw that the gully had opened out; the surrounding mountains seemed less rugged and there was a narrow, flat space on both sides of the river. The water seemed to be flowing more calmly and the white-capped ripples had disappeared from its surface. The pilot asked Tajil, as the man in charge, if it would be all right to land somewhere around there. After a brief exchange with us, Tajil gave him the OK sign.

The helicopter dropped down until it was almost skimming the water, moving slowly forward in search of a flat piece of ground. Within three minutes the pilot had found a suitable-looking place and lowered the skids gently some twenty yards from the river, raising a cloud of dust. We had landed. I got out first and stood on the firm ground while Tajil and Pierre prepared to hand things out to me. Since goods as well as people had to be unloaded, the pilot switched off the engine and got out as well. Several cardboard boxes, the dinghy and the crated outboard motor were handed down to us. The whole operation took about fifteen minutes. Then the helicopter took off again, leaving the three of us behind.

At the spot we'd chosen the riverbed was about a hundred yards wide and, although the cliffs on both sides were still precipitous, the river itself meandered peacefully along the middle of the bed, suggesting that somewhere not too far upstream the ground did indeed become a wide plateau. When we looked back at the way we'd come, the cliffs seemed to be virtually leaning toward each other and we realized just how little space the pilot had had to maneuver in.

I sat down on a large stone.

"How long will we have to wait?" Pierre asked of no one in particular.

"Four or five hours," Tajil said. "All we'll be able to do today, anyway, is just get everything and everybody here and the camp set up. We could sort out some of the supplies, I suppose." And he started lining up the boxes as he spoke.

"What kind of bird is that?" I asked, pointing at a small black shadow in the sky.

"It's big. Probably an eagle," said Pierre. Tajil didn't look up, but just went on with what he was doing.

"I didn't expect to see an eagle in a place like this."

"The whole region belongs to him. All of this is his."

"What does he live on, I wonder?"

"There must be small animals here—rabbits, lizards. And then of course there are other birds."

We heard the noise of the helicopter again shortly after three o'clock. First we heard the engine, then we caught a glimpse of something moving in the shadow of the cliffs, lost it in deeper shadow, then saw it again as the roar of the engine drew rapidly closer and at last, like a bee loaded with honey, the helicopter flew suddenly into the light. The yellow jacket I'd taken off was nearby and I stood up and signaled with it.

At that precise moment, a dark shadow seemed to fall from the upper air toward the helicopter. It could have been just my imagination, I suppose, yet when I strained my eyes to try to make out what it was, the helicopter suddenly wobbled, lurched sideways, went into a spin and crashed into the cliff. For a second it was impossible to believe it had really happened. The helicopter was still at an altitude of three to four hundred feet when it hit the cliff, exploding in a ball of orange flame where it struck, then disintegrating as it started falling. The roar of the explosion burst inside our stomachs as we stood there watching in horror. The main body of the helicopter flared up again when it hit the ground, and one or two small fragments drifted down on it.

We raced toward the wreckage, stumbling over stones and clambering over rocks, but the helicopter had crashed on the far bank and the river was running too high for us to cross. Pierre waded impetuously into it, but it wasn't shallow enough for fording so Tajil and I pulled him back. All the three of us could do was stand at the water's edge and watch the fire blazing only a few dozen yards away. We went on watching to see if anyone emerged from the wreck, but no one did. A strong stench of fuel, charred metal and other smells of burning drifted over to us across the water. We felt the heat on our faces as the helicopter continued to burn for another ten or fifteen minutes, as if it were determined to show that there had been an accident. Then only the blackened wreck remained, licked by an occasional tongue of flame.

After a while Tajil recovered enough presence of mind to start inflating the dinghy. We crossed the river to the scene of the disaster, not because we thought there was anything we could do, but merely as a gesture. Everything had been incinerated and the smell was appalling. Scattered all around were pieces of twisted metal and a number of scorched and smoldering objects, from which blue smoke still rose. We thought the four corpses would be in the biggest piece of wreckage, right in the middle, but it was still too hot to get close. There was absolutely nothing we could do.

Although this was an exploratory trip we were on, it certainly wasn't the kind that could be described as hazardous. We weren't being asked to make a winter crossing of Antarctica on foot. It wasn't even a full-scale scientific expedition, as our task was only to ascertain the existence of a specific site and find out more or less what it was. So we might have expected one of us to break a leg or something, but nobody could possibly have foreseen that we would lose half our party in a single instant and that the three survivors would be left stranded, with no means of getting back.

That night we lit our fire on the other side of the river, as far away from the scene of the disaster as possible, and prepared a simple meal even though no one felt hungry. Then we sat and stared silently into the flames. Tajil said he intended to sit tight until rescuers arrived and, up until that moment, I'd been thinking along the same lines. When the helicopter didn't return to its base that night, another one would be sent to look for us, within a few days at most. Even if, for some reason, that didn't happen, at least the committee in Paris that had organized the expedition and my television company in Tokyo could be counted on to get some sort of research operation under way. We had food, and our surroundings didn't look particularly dangerous, so the best option would be just to wait.

But even while all this was being spelled out, it occurred to me that we might just as well push on with our investigation of the Oneiros site. Obviously, after an accident in which half our party had been killed, nobody would blame us if we called the whole thing off, but we had already come this far and it was only a fairly short journey to our objective. At least we could find out if the place was an authentic ruin or just an accident of nature.

When I thought about it later, I could come up with no reason why I should have tried so hard to get the others to share this point of view. It wasn't any motive of company loyalty that moved me, no desire to fulfill my mission, no urge to achieve something before I returned home. The only thing that concerned me was to shorten the distance between where I was now and where the site lay, as quickly and surely as possible. Maybe it was just that I disliked the idea of waiting here within sight of the burned wreckage of the helicopter. Most things become harder to understand the farther you get from them. All important decisions are made on the spur of the moment, but we forget the true motives of the mind and heart that lie behind them.

Tajil opposed my plan. No matter what I said, he continued to insist that we stay and wait to be rescued. What he really wanted, he said, was to get out of here, to take the dinghy and go back downstream, but since that was impossible we would just have to wait. In his view, going on into the interior with just the three of us and so few provisions was completely insane.

Pierre couldn't make up his mind. Even I had no intention of going on by myself to look for the site, and if Pierre had said he was staying behind I would have had no choice but to follow suit. He said that his inclination was to press on, but added in a low voice that there was one aspect of the present situation that made him hesitate, though he declined to say what it was. We decided to give him until morning to work out what he wanted to do, and the three of us climbed into our sleeping bags. It was bitterly cold that night, but I don't think that's why I found it so hard to sleep. What kept me awake was the sheer inexplicability of the accident, combined with anxiety over what we were going to do next. I could hear gentle snores coming from Tajil's sleeping bag while I lay there thinking I would never get to sleep. But, as it happened, I had reached the limits of fatigue. By the time I became aware of my surroundings again it was already morning and the sun was lighting up the gorge.

As I was getting up, Pierre spoke to me from his sleeping bag.

"I'll go with you," he said.

10

From the day we first heard the music, we devoted all our daylight hours simply to wandering about the site. How many days that lasted I'm not really sure. We camped on the river-bank, waking each morning eager to resume, eating a quick breakfast or even making do with a little water before heading back up the gully. Once there, we would separate to walk around or just sit on a stone listening for the voices, that music, those wordless messages. Sometimes we would make desperate efforts to transmit our own thoughts to the presence that hov-ered there. At least, that's what I remember trying to do, but whether I spoke or merely concentrated on stimulating some mental energy, whether I gestured, stamped or even danced in that square of stones, I can't recall. Those kinds of details are so utterly absent from my memory it's as though someone had deliberately erased them.

Sometimes the two of us would sit together for a long time in the square. There would be a complete rapport between us then. To an observer, we would just have looked like two young men sitting in silence, but those were the times when the understanding between us was deepest. The important thing was that while we were together, we had a multiple insight into the connections between humanity and whatever it was that the site stood for. We represented two separate vantage points, for our characters were completely different; yet that very difference created a dual scan, a way of really measuring the distance between our world and that other one and, eventually perhaps, of judging whether the gulf could be crossed. Things wouldn't have turned out as they did, I think, if only one of us had gone to the site.

But what actually happened there? What messages did the site send us? I can't say. I can't express it in ordinary language, the language of this world. All I can do is hesitate, and say I no longer understand. We heard music there. The music was more than just voices and sounds reaching us from outside; it came from inside us as well. It was like your own voice rising within you—not the voice of your ego, nothing as trivial as that, but the real self, that microcosm which includes all living things. If I were forced to put it into words, I would say it was like listening to the sound of the blood inside your ears, to the billions of pulses per second flying between the cells of your brain, to the tiny creaking sounds the bones and joints of the body make when they are so perfectly lubricated that they work almost noiselessly, to the rustling of the cells of the whole body. It was as if this whole process had become transparent. In the stirring of the genes, the passage of time itself became visible—that vast expanse traversed by all individual beings since life began. And then you saw all that preceded life, saw across that immense tract of time to the beginning of everything: the dance of atoms as they changed, the brightening of the universe, the explosions of great stars and the flowing forth of the very stuff of life, the birth of nebulae and planets, including this planet, and finally the cooling of the surface of the earth and the birth of life forms in its oceans. To listen to that music was to hear these processes, to absorb them like things physically experienced.

Amid all this, the self did not exist. I was not myself and

Pierre was not Pierre. We were diffused throughout a space that wasn't only vast but still expanding, and we filled the whole of it. Our bodies felt as though they stretched to the very edge of the world. We weren't simply the sum total of all living things— far more than that: we were existence itself. We had escaped from the well of the ego at last, scattered in all directions, filling the universe.

When the wind blew, I could hear that sound. The motion of each particle of air carrying the sound I experienced as the rustling of my own cells. Through that movement, the site, like a relay station, transmitted to me the joy of my own existence. There was no need to peer around outside myself, for I was both looking and being looked at. I was a self observing myself, the viewer and the viewed, the clouds and the blue sky. I was the great eagle that sliced through the air and the man sitting on the stone whom the eagle looked down on. I was the man who danced and the boy who lay on the ground sleeping with outstretched arms, and whose arms, as he slept, became the wings of the soaring eagle.

I had no need to be myself. I didn't have to act always as a specific person among strangers whom one treated with the utmost wariness. I was no longer required to be a man of his time, a man with adequate physical and mental skills, who spoke Japanese and passable English and had a decent grasp of mathematics, who had opinions on current affairs, could support himself and had some capacity for judgment, a man with a socially acceptable level of intelligence: in short, an individual personality acknowledged by other people. I didn't have to be that young Japanese man with the above-average ability to get his own way, since the effort to perform that particular role and to sustain it as long as other people were around had become entirely irrelevant. This didn't mean I would be enjoying some idle Sunday of the spirit where one lolled about at home in scruffy pajamas, having given up the struggle for a while. It meant that, since I now coexisted with everything, I was freed from any obligation to make and remake myself. My thoughts could be transmitted to others unhampered by that perpetual concern with what was being thought of me. While I wasn't even conscious that it was happening, my thoughts would be spreading in waves throughout the world and linking up with other waves from countless other epicenters, waves that met to form a single grand design, the splendid arabesque of the universe.

Alongside me, Pierre was going through an almost identical experience, I knew that. We were two overlapping, nearly concentric circles, our centers only a fraction apart, twin sources of consciousness transmitting in the same bipolar moment. His face was mine and he shared my body, unaltered. His entire past was my past, along with the past, present and future of all human beings, from the mothers of the Neanderthals to the newest-born baby. I could sense them all in me; and yet I was still myself. I never stopped being aware that I was myself. That was the difference between Pierre and me.

How many days did we spend like that? I don't know. All I know is that, as the light faded and the narrow strip of sky above the gully darkened, we stumbled away from the place like a pair of music students at the end of a grueling day at the piano. Usually we left at the same time; sometimes one of us had to wait for the other, but never for long. Clearly there was some accord between us, but whether it was something we communicated directly to each other or something the site transmitted to both of us equally through the great eagle, neither of us knew. Anyway, we would arrive at the entrance to the site almost simultaneously, as if at some agreed time, and make our way back down the gully together.

We gradually stopped eating normal amounts of food. Eating had lost its appeal. From the time we got back to camp until we went to sleep we were busy enough just going over the things we'd experienced during the day. But we were like children who had been set too much homework, or given too big a piece of cake to eat, because as we tried to relive those emotions we would find ourselves unable to make sense of anything, and before we knew it we'd be asleep. To say that one can be aware of being in a state of unawareness is absurd, I know, but in this case it is a fair description of how we felt.

Just once I woke up unusually early. Not wanting to disturb Pierre, I went to the river and started fishing. There was some basic fishing gear among our stores, and on our trip up the river I'd thought I'd like to try it out one day. Now I remembered it. Since the kit wasn't for any particular kind of fish, it had as many as thirty different flies and hooks, but, presumably because the river had never been fished and the fish didn't know what was going on, I caught one with my first fly. In fact I had a bite with almost every cast and had caught five trout-like fish before I knew it.

Back at the camp, Pierre had just got up. I showed him my catch and we decided to have it for breakfast. The fish tasted delicious, and I'd actually enjoyed catching them, but we both had the peculiar feeling that we were somehow eating ourselves. I'd experienced something like it on the riverbank: a feeling that I had become the river and was flowing with it, that two separate things were merging. It was as if the walls of our selves had fallen down and nothing separated us from our surroundings. The fish had been part of us, they had left us, and now they had returned. If that was really how things were, the act of eating—however good the taste—seemed a lot less compelling.

The result, in any case, was that we ate no more fish.

11

"I was in love once," said Pierre, about three days after we'd arrived at the stronghold, if that's what it was. We were sitting by the fire at our camp near the river, trying to make sense of the confused impressions of the day, half lost in reverie.

"We were in the same year at university. She was a wonderful girl, and I went out of my way to get to know her. We sat next to each other at lectures and talked for hours in cafes. I sketched her face as she sat on a bench in the park and took her home by the most roundabout route. Every day I would plan how we could spend as much time together as possible. The better I got to know her the more I loved her. We'd both been born on a Saturday—little things like that were nice. I suppose it's the same with everybody. None of the other girls in the class meant anything to me—they were grass in the meadow; I barely saw them as individuals. Just this one flower, that's all I saw. She was the one brilliant spot of color in a black and white photograph.

"Then one day, by which time we'd become very close, she told me she had a boyfriend. But she didn't, for that reason, say she couldn't see me any more. She didn't ask me to forget her. She liked me and didn't think it would be wrong to go on just as we were, enjoying each other's company. She said she'd be happy if things could continue. And she said this in all inno-cence. She wasn't playing any tricks, or being greedy; she was simply following her heart. As for me, I had no intention of let-ting this stop me from seeing her. I didn't ask her to choose between the two of us, either.

"So we went on as before, going to movies and plays together, eating in this or that little place we'd found, sometimes taking long walks in the country. She hardly ever mentioned the boyfriend, and she never once told me, now that I knew about him, how much she liked him, what sort of relationship they had, how often she met him or what he did. I suppose if I'd insisted she would have told me, but I wasn't prepared to take the risk. I imagined he was probably some graduate student, but I didn't really care who or what he was. I loved her so much that I was afraid if I asked too much I might lose her. Also I was a coward. I had this fear that if I knew too much about him he would become real to me, sharp and clear enough to cause me pain.

"This may sound unbelievable in the case of a young man and woman both around twenty, but right from the start I hardly laid a finger on her. In fact I never really thought that our relationship would go in that direction. The idea of sleeping together seemed so ordinary it was almost distasteful, like setting up some fake household. I felt that way from previous experience. I also thought that if all I wanted was a girl to sleep with, I could always find one if I tried. But she was special, absolutely special. When I think about it now, I can see an element of sour grapes in all that, but at the time I honestly believed she was different from other girls, perhaps because that notion was all I had to cling to. I despised the body, the flesh. I convinced myself that her very existence was so special she was above such things. I also decided not to think about the question of whether she was sleeping with her boyfriend or not.

"The truth is, of course, that going to bed with her was a gamble, for stakes I thought I couldn't afford. But any normal man would have made that bet, wouldn't he?"

As he said this he looked at me, but I didn't reply, simply urging him to go on with his story.

"So it was enough to hold her hand and kiss her briefly. It was an expression of intimacy and nothing more. And it was wonderful, that intimacy, it really was—I'm not exaggerating. I held her hand and thought that if I could feel as close to her as this, what need was there to sleep with her?

"But it was no good. I started to feel ashamed of my own feebleness. Close friendship isn't like passionate love; it shouldn't be an ego trip, it should be steady, unchanging. What I was feeling therefore couldn't be called that. I knew only too well that one part of me wanted very badly to be fully merged with her, inside the same cocoon, to be naked and to hold her, oblivious of time, to press my face into every nook and cranny of her body. I knew that I should be trying to move things along in some way that would lead to this goal, but in fact I did nothing. I chose to go on believing that I was happy just to hold her hand and that I shouldn't even think about any other aspect of her body. You'll think that's childish, no doubt."

He looked at me questioningly, but I shook my head.

"But it was. I was still young, immature. I still believed that a simple, logical argument could win out over my real self. At least I tried to believe that, but the self isn't quite so easily deceived. I was perfectly aware I was suffering from feelings of jealousy and that they were very painful feelings indeed. It would have been strange if I hadn't been aware of it, since it's not possible to suffer an emotion and not actually feel it, and I certainly felt my jealousy. While I was talking to her the shadow of this invisible man would fall between us. She tried to avoid mentioning him, but sometimes we'd be talking about a subject that seemed somehow to hint at him, and for a second he would appear, then just as quickly disappear again. But she was so pure! Her face, her voice, her heart; it was all pure, all beautiful.

"Once she had her hair cut in a new style. It looked so fresh and lovely it was as if some unseen hands—cherubs' hands, if you like—were behind her, holding it like that. But, just as I was about to say something to that effect, everything suddenly went dark. You see, there *was* somebody behind her, somebody I didn't know. You know how in an eclipse both the sun and the moon are in the earth's shadow? Well, someone was hidden behind her just like that. When *I* thought her hair was lovely, *he* was thinking exactly the same thing. Anyone who looked at her with the eyes of love was bound to think so. Maybe it had happened only an hour ago, or yesterday, maybe it was going to happen in two hours' time, or tomorrow. And seeing her hair shining in the sunlight, I felt she was moving away from me, going steadily farther away, receding and receding toward a place where I wouldn't be able to reach her any more, and I'd be left there alone. Can you understand that?"

I nodded vigorously.

"It was always the same. She quite innocently enjoyed the time she spent with me, and no doubt she enjoyed the time she spent with the other man just as innocently. Yet I never had the feeling that she must be comparing us, though that didn't make the situation any less painful. As I said, it was like an eclipse, in which this lovely planet passed between me and another body. As long as I was with her, this was what I'd have to put up with.

"Yes, I know, it's a common enough story. It's probably been repeated billions of times throughout history. Think about it: all confessions, all confidences, all kinds of novels, all popular songs boil down to this same situation. Gorillas and lions and whales in the icy oceans probably go through the same agonies in their dealings with the opposite sex. Maybe even plane trees, dandelions, mushrooms, those rare cells that Pasteur discovered, cold viruses and things like that all suffer in exactly the same way.

"Anyway, as time went on I came to feel a weird kind of

empathy with this shadowy figure I'd never met. He was another version of myself, the other side of me. I had never even seen him. I suppose I may have come across him without knowing it, though even someone as guileless as she was probably made sure that would never happen. I had no idea what sort of person he might be, I only knew he was a dark reflection of me.

"Then an idea suddenly came to me. If I could somehow link myself to his circuit, if we were joined by a single cable and an attempt at some kind of emotional communication were made, then there could be an exchange between two comrades in love. His joys could be communicated to me and mine to him, and the love we had in common would be love equally shared. If that proved possible, all this futile suffering would disappear.

"I felt at that moment the pointlessness of the competition that the two of us, each trapped within himself, were keeping up. I saw our situation from the outside, and it made me realize that we were the victims of a preposterous trick, an elaborate game whose every rule we obeyed. We were shut inside ourselves—not just the two of us, but everybody. We were all urged to compete, given incentives to compete. We were each at the bottom of a tiny bucket, swung crazily right and left and left and right, slaves to that insane motion. That's all it was. And yet if only we could jump out of the bucket, there was a vast and beautiful world, a world of freedom, waiting for us.

"To link up with my rival, to plug into him, would mean making one little hole in the bucket to pass the wire through. Once that was done, all the joy that he experienced could be transmitted to me and life, with all its usual trials, would change. Why not, why couldn't this be arranged? Who had thought up this system of constant competition and imposed it on us, on all the creatures of the world, all equally the victims of this fraud?

"Anyway, what happened next? Well, the girl and I finally broke up. This love masquerading as friendship lasted about a year, then we both got a bit tired of it. Or you could say, there was no clear desire on her part to move on to another stage, to enter the cocoon, and I didn't have the courage to push for it. The shadow man stayed in the shadows. When at the end of that time I went to a provincial university for a year, I made that my excuse for leaving her. I suppose we'd both outgrown each other, but who knows? Maybe if the other man hadn't existed— this man I called a shadow and whom I'd thought of linking up with somehow—if he hadn't been there things might have gone on longer. Maybe we would have lived together. We might have married and had children by now. I suppose as far as she was concerned I was the person she could most readily open her heart to. I don't imagine she'd ever been as close to anyone as she was to me. The fact that I then accepted the existence of another party, in this lunar eclipse type of arrangement I told you about, just shows how bad I am at relationships. So that's my love story, the story of a good-hearted fool in love.

"But you know, if that's all it was, it would just have been an episode that could have happened to anyone. In my case, though, it was a little more serious than that, a little more significant. For me it turned into something representative of every kind of human relationship. Thinking about it afterward, I realized that even before it started I was already on the defensive. There was something lacking in me. I wasn't prepared to follow the competitive ethic, to hide inside the fortress of myself and shoot arrows at a distant enemy or throw stones at him or write him long, threatening letters. I didn't seem to have the will to win by such methods. In fact I didn't play any game that involved winning and losing. I didn't like the idea of losing myself and I didn't like the idea of making someone else lose, either.

So I just hung about not knowing what to do, standing back and making way for the other person, then following unhappily after him, but never overtaking him at places where I should have gone ahead.

"I kept thinking how nice it would be if there were no such thing as struggle in the world, if things had been distributed equally beforehand. I thought how easy it would be if there were no distinction between myself and other people, if we all felt our sensations in common, if we all became a single living organism. I wished the shadow man and I could be linked up by that cable, not so we could each have the same girl but so we could both fall back, equally and at the same time, and then combine. The idea of our separate selves would fade while the consciousness of us together deepened.

"I've gone on thinking in that way. I've spent my days reflecting on things I can't discuss with anyone, because in the eyes of this vigorous, censorious society of ours I would look like a defector, a dropout, a nobody. Perhaps I am one."

"Linkage is not allowed," I said. "Connecting people with cables offends the concept of impartiality. It would infringe the anti-monopoly laws. It would impose a restriction on fair, legitimate competition."

"It's the competitive ethic I don't accept."

"And what you were after was a reverse transaction, a deal worked out behind the scenes, if you like," I said. "You were supposed to be in love with the girl, not the man, and the idea of shared happiness with someone you don't love makes no sense. Anyway, all individual entities are in opposition to one another. This is something that precedes ethics; it's the first principle of existence. The fundamental idea behind the universe is that of competition."

"All right," said Pierre. "But suppose that idea is restricted only to our planet? Suppose the whole box of tricks only applies on this star, that we're the only ones who've fallen for this swindle en masse? Who's to say this isn't the one place in the universe that relies on your principle, the one star where the sense of existence is shut up inside each individual so that we're all forced to struggle with one another? I see no reason why not, or why all those nebulae out there shouldn't share each other's thoughts perfectly and live in total harmony."

"You've taken the argument to such heights I've lost track of it," I said. "Anyway, it's pointless making statements that can't be proved. Let's restrict the argument to what goes on here on earth. If you and that man had been able to achieve some kind of joint possession of your girlfriend, her appeal would have vanished instantly. Her real attraction wasn't just inherent; it was the product of a competition she's in with all the other women in the world. You yourself became the person you are by a constant process of improving yourself through competition with other men, other colleagues and, by extension, with all human beings. You measured yourself against other people and worked out how to get ahead of them. If it hadn't been for all those competitors, all those millions of other men, you would've got tired of her right away. You probably wouldn't even have been attracted to her in the first place, and she wouldn't ever have looked at you. The idea of one heart linking up with others and everyone sharing their happiness comes from a loser in the war between individuals, someone who's fled the battlefield.

"And what about linking up with the girl, never mind the shadow man? If you'd ever managed that, she would virtually have become yourself. But how can you fall in love with yourself? How can you make love to yourself? Her whole heart and mind would have been revealed to you, like looking down at a landscape from a plane and seeing everything laid out. What sort of love do you call that?"

Pierre didn't respond; he just looked silently into the darkness, toward the site at the end of the gully. Obviously he hadn't accepted my simpleminded argument. It was hardly likely that he would.

12

When I draw arabesques on Kent paper I am attempting to restore (if only on paper) the order that this world has lost, and I enjoy that, even though I've failed as yet to make the face of God appear in them. Doing it is very close to the experience of sitting among those stones and listening. The drawback is that everything is on a horizontal plane, extending to a limited horizon. I wonder if I'd be satisfied if I could do it in three dimensions, with minute, intricately linked containers of thin, transparent glass, filled with varicolored gases? No, I doubt it.

What I'm looking for is not something complete and self-contained, whether in a two- or three-dimensional form, but something that connects over a much wider area, operating like a small transmitter. The patterns I draw, the colors I fill in between the lines, would be converted into messages sent out into space. I am here, they would say, I am in the here and now, but what I want is to dissolve, to be absorbed into everything else. I want to be everywhere at the same time, to see everything, to rejoice in everything. That is the message I'd like to send.

The site was probably the one place on earth where it was possible to communicate with the upper world, where messages from a world transcending the one we know could be received. Think of it as a relay station for the universal mind.

If I had to choose a metaphor to describe it—something I never even thought of doing at the time—I would choose a first-floor elevator door. Pierre and I stood before the door and watched intently as the lights indicating the various floors went on and off. On the upper floors were Andromeda Junction and Seifert's Galaxy, the source of supernovas, midnight black holes and Ylem Point. The question was, when the elevator came, would we get on or not? The sign would light up, the door would open and pause, but would we take that step inside?

We went on waiting for that moment, unable to make up our minds.

13

The music of Oneiros was a whirlpool of all possible sounds, full of voices, each one distinct even though they were in perfect unison. I heard the voices of old friends, the voice of my dead father, of a singer I used to like and had completely forgotten, of the helicopter pilot who had just died, the thunder of a waterfall hidden deep in the Andes and as yet unheard by human ears, whales singing in the Antarctic Ocean, all the crickets in the world, one by one, and the sound made by every grain of sand sifting past other sand. And I heard my own voice as a child, as Pierre once said he had.

Yet, in the end, my experience and Pierre's were different, fundamentally so. I heard the voice of my childhood self, but it didn't speak to me directly. I simply heard the voice, because all I did was listen. I didn't speak, I didn't sing. At night, when we returned to camp and sat around the fire, talking briefly every now and then about the day's experiences, Pierre's comments always concerned conversations he'd had. Mine tended to suggest I'd been listening to a concert. The people Pierre had these conversations with were never specified; it was more like a thou- sand people engaging with another thousand via a million dif- ferent channels, with him possessing one of the sets of a thousand voices. And I should have realized this could only mean one thing: that he'd been drawn into the greater world where the music originated, had entered the state in which sep- arate identities all merge. He'd taken the step inside the eleva- tor.

We now ate practically nothing. When we woke up in the morning our bodies were already in a state of perfect readiness, and a single mouthful of water saw us through a whole day at the site. We said very little to each other. The shared experience of the place had given us a sense of ultimate intimacy; it was as though, having crossed a certain line, we appeared to each other as transparent and insubstantial as air. Oneiros had come to mean a language not made of everyday words, a logic without structure, invisible images. Through these things it taught us about the nature of the universe, the unfolding of space time and how we could enter it. Nobody did this for us. It was simply a matter of standing on the brink of total being and looking at what could be seen there. That privilege was given to us, that was all, and we spent our time there absorbed in what we saw.

In due course, though, I began to sense a change in us two. Whereas I was standing my ground, hesitating to go on, Pierre had unconsciously entered new territory and was moving far- ther and farther into it. Perhaps this was a gauge of the differ- ence in our characters, or perhaps the place itself had chosen between us and was now fostering that difference. But some- thing had changed.

My eyes seemed to be gradually opening. The site exercised the same power over me during the day and I was still entranced

by the sounds, in which I continued to float like a large nebu-
la—at least that's how it felt. But when we returned to our
camp at night and sat in silence by the fire looking at the
flames, I experienced more than once a kind of shocked realization that this wasn't a place where I belonged. There was something utterly wrong about the whole thing, although where the
mistake lay I had no idea. Somewhere in the middle of a long,
long calculation, an error had occurred, but I couldn't pinpoint
it. Finally, on one of these occasions, while I was sitting there
wondering what to do, I looked at Pierre and said suddenly,
before I was even aware I was saying it:

"Let's go back."

"What?" he said in amazement, as if this were the last thing
he ever expected to hear.

"Let's just go. This isn't the kind of place anyone should stay
too long."

As soon as I'd spoken, I realized where the error lay. I knew
now what was wrong.

"Why?"

"I think this is a kind of trap, a trap for people's minds. It
takes them captive. It leads them away to a different world."

Pierre didn't reply for a while.

"You may be right," he said at last. "Perhaps we *are* being
lured into it. But suppose it led to somewhere people ought to
go?"

"There's no such place. There's nowhere else we could live
but here on earth."

"I don't agree."

"Then you're wrong. What we're being tempted to believe is
that there's another way of life, not living wrapped up in our
private selves but sharing one existence. And yet the only way
we *can* live is enclosed like that, inside ourselves. That's what

life is. The essential condition of life."

"But there's no competition here," said Pierre. "Or rather, in the greater world that starts from here there's no distinction between oneself and others. From the moment I was born right up to now, I've always felt utterly alone—shut up at the top of a high tower, with everybody else shut up inside theirs. Even if I shouted at the top of my voice, no one could hear. I used to think, if only we could all come down from our towers and hug and hold hands and dance in the fields below. But nobody knows the way down. Now, after coming here, I've realized at last that the primordial mistake was to separate life into these individual existences. Everything should be interconnected in a single, harmonious state. Somebody, or something, introduced the principle of individual rivalry on this planet—and nowhere else—in order to conduct an experiment in the accelerated evolution of forms of life. It was an appalling mistake, and we're the ones who've been paying for it, with incalculable misery. The life force isn't meant for such brief periods of existence, such perpetual anxiety, such irrepressible feelings of loss. And that's the fact of it."

"You sound as if you're trying to convince yourself. All I suggested was that we go back."

"I'm trying to explain to you the reason I won't be going with you. Why do people console themselves with religion? Because they're alone, because they're all in their solitary towers looking down at the fields below. They want to go down, but there's no way there. The only way of getting out is to jump, which means jumping to one's death. People want an end to strife, to live in harmony and peace, and with that in view they've come up with any number of religious ideas; the trouble is, none of them is very effective. What these people want is what we've experienced here, the sense of being linked to every minute particle of matter in the world, a sense that one's feelings are shared by everything that lives. Isn't that so?

"Look, we've been chosen. On what basis I don't know, but chosen we have been. Those who aren't ready can't come here. Why the choice had to be made in as violent a way as that helicopter crash I don't know either. Maybe it really was just an accident. But now the two of us are here. We don't even need food any more. There's no reason why this shouldn't continue forever. It's a state anybody would envy us—everybody wants to be where we are now. Why should we go back?"

"Because we're human beings, that's why," I said. "Certainly I'm happy, much more than happy, to have been given this glimpse of the world on the other side. But that doesn't alter the absolute condition that's governed all life on this earth since the very beginning: of being alone, being segregated. However strong the temptation, we can't escape it. You said it yourself, the only way to reach the world outside the tower is through death. Your wanting to stay here, in fact, is just a death wish."

"You're wrong. Can't you feel it yourself—this growing sense of integration? We've found a relay station—a route that gets us to the other side without having to pass through death."

"It's *dis*integration in your case. You're being consumed. The things you're made of are slowly being broken down, to be re-used in the 'whole' you talk about."

"Everything you say proves that you can only see things from the standpoint of the ego. You talk in terms of 'uses' and 'purposes,' but it's all beside the point. The individual 'I' isn't being used to serve the purposes of the whole. The whole isn't like some enormous individual. The whole is simply everything. The whole is. And the fact that it is is sufficient reason for it."

I remained silent. I felt as if every temptation experienced by man since human life began lay spread out before my eyes. If you believed that man was what he was because he had reached a higher point than where he started, whether one called it a lonely tower or not, then anything that tried to draw him down again was a temptation to be anti-human. Whether Oneiros was a trap made by angels or devils, it was a temptation to abandon the flesh we were made of and it had to be resisted. To give up one's humanity, even if it was to achieve some higher state of being, was a breach of the contract made when we were born on this earth ...

But none of this would get through to Pierre. It was nothing but words, mere arguments, stiff and unyielding. Such was the power of this place, in fact, I only half believed them myself, letting them circle idly in my mind. Pierre didn't say any more either, but got into his sleeping bag. Almost at once I heard his quiet breathing. We were at the stage where, fulfilled by the events of the day, we tended to fall very quickly into a deep sleep. Most evenings when I got into my sleeping bag I would instantly lose all sense of where I was, but that night, probably because of my resistance to the effect of the site, I couldn't sleep. I lay there wondering if I really would leave Pierre on his own. Since coming here our lives had grown oddly abstracted. We hardly ate anything, scarcely felt the heat or cold. Apart from the occasional discussion such as we'd just been having, nearly all our waking hours were filled with music and nothing else. Was it right to leave him to go on like this while I returned alone?

I liked Pierre. This wasn't an effect of the affinity the place brought out in us (or at least I didn't believe it was). I liked him because I felt at ease with him in various ways. For someone like me, who usually found it difficult to get on with people, this had turned out to be an unusually strong friendship. I didn't want to leave him here. I realized that doing so would be the same in the end as leaving him to die. It would mean abandoning him to a dreadful, lingering suicide.

Maybe, I decided, I should tie him up inside his sleeping bag and take him downstream by force. If I got the rope around him quickly enough he'd be unable to put up much resistance; then I could heave him into the dinghy, start the engine and set off. Even a short distance from the site, we might find ourselves free of its influence and able to think and behave normally again. But if he really believed that the site was trying to save us, it would look as if I were the one not willing to listen to reason, behaving like a willful child. Was it really Pierre who was the good boy and I the rebel?

Though still uncertain on this point, I made up my mind to carry out my rescue plan. But just as I was slipping out of my sleeping bag, I looked in his direction. To my astonishment, I saw that his body was glowing; the light it gave off was actually shining through his sleeping bag. My whole frame went rigid—all I could do was stare. His body gradually blazed even brighter, seeming to grow larger as well, and then began to rise into the air, slowly and still horizontal, while he went on sleeping. At the same time it became more and more transparent, like the figure of a young god made of fine green-blue glass. It kept rising, stage by stage, into the air. I watched, spellbound. When he was so high I had to look up at him, I could see stars shining through his body, as if it were expanding to embrace the night and to be embraced, the more rarefied and extended it grew. And then, much farther off—a single dazzling point of light in the distant darkness—I saw the eagle flying.

I thought I was the victim of an hallucination, something that wasn't really happening at all. Yet, even if this were an illusion, I took it as a sort of preview, made possible by some minute adjustment of the time scale, of what was actually going to take place in a few days', or a few years', time. Perhaps the site itself was trying to show me what was in store for him if he stayed there. Perhaps it was showing me the basic difference between myself and Pierre. Any number of ideas tumbled through my head, and my mind stood still, lost among them.

After a while the image grew so fine in the air it simply melted away. But when I looked over at Pierre's sleeping bag again, there he was, sleeping quietly as usual. I decided not to take him with me.

The next morning I told him I was going back alone. He didn't comment. I asked him pointedly if it was all right for me to take the rubber dinghy, since it was the only boat we had, and he nodded. He seemed to have decided not to speak. I divided the provisions in two, left him those things I thought he might be able to use, and loaded mine on board. Then I went up to him.

"Shall I come back to get you?" I asked.

"You'd better not. The place isn't right for you," he said in a low, hoarse voice.

I took him by the shoulders and hugged him. There were tears in my eyes. I suppressed the other things I wanted to say and walked to the edge of the river without looking back, then climbed into the dinghy and pushed off. After a little while I did look back and saw him standing on the riverbank, waving. I waved back at him. That was the last I saw of him, standing there on the bank, waving his hand, silhouetted against the sky.

So I went down the river we had traveled up together. By the second day I was back at the place where the helicopter had crashed. I stood on the bank and saw that Tajil wasn't there, but a little way back from the river I noticed a withered tree with a piece of red cloth tied to it, and under the tree was a radio set, carefully boxed and packaged against the unlikely event of rain. It was the kind where you just wound a handle to operate it and had probably been part of the emergency kit of the helicopter that had come to rescue Tajil. I used it to contact the airport at Kabul, and was picked up without any fuss the next day.

After that I was asked to explain why only I had returned and not Pierre. I was asked to explain what sort of place the site was, whether I thought it was of human or natural origin, and how many days I'd spent there. I was asked to explain everything, but I answered none of the questions.

14

Since I began seriously putting all this down in writing, I haven't drawn any more arabesques. I should have done more than 180 by now, and it's possible, I suppose, that in one of them the patterns and colors might have come together perfectly and the face of God appeared. But I've been lazy about that experiment recently. Perhaps it wouldn't be the God I ought to meet. What I need to think about next is some way of getting in touch with the human race again. I have to find a road that will lead me back to the world of other men.

If I show the doctor what I've written, I should be able to speak again. That's one way. Showing it would almost certainly get me out of here. The doctor would pronounce me psychologically normal, capable of conversation with other people, someone who can lead a normal life in accordance with the standards of society. I'd be able to go back to my old job with the television company. I know that what I've recorded here is an extraordinary experience, but it's written in plain language and with a clear enough conscience, so anyone who reads it should be able to understand me, even if Pierre's behavior is beyond them. It can serve as a farewell to Pierre and a declaration of my wish to return to society.

But I'm still hesitating. What I've put down is for myself; it wasn't meant for others' eyes. I wrote it in secret, so other people wouldn't know about it. Whenever I left my room I would hide the manuscript in a drawer underneath my 156 arabesques. I wrote it to put my own experiences in order. I'm like a child who has done his homework but feels no confidence in it and is reluctant to show it to his teacher.

One reason for this reluctance is that I can still hear the music. Even today I can hear it. The clinic has musak playing everywhere, but the sounds of Oneiros are always in my ears and drown it out. I first noticed them right after I got back—heard them all the time in fact, so that I was unable to hear anything else around me. It happened while they were questioning me, probing so persistently when I couldn't manage to reply that I lost consciousness; and when to all appearances I was sound asleep and even the EEG showed I was in a coma, I heard the sounds more clearly still. Then the longing to be back there with Pierre filled my chest so that I could hardly breathe. I remembered every detail of each day I spent there—how long it all seemed now!—and in my heart I wept. I wanted to return to those days, walk along that stony road, look up at the great bird overhead, see those torn, scarred cliffs, drink the river water; and as all those memories flooded through me I was helpless. I could do nothing. When my eyes opened on my present emptiness, the sense of loss I felt was almost unendurable.

Even now, at this moment, I feel something close to that, for the music has suddenly begun to fill my mind again. My experience at Oneiros was so overwhelming that I've had great trouble turning the whole thing into something I can cope with. I've been thinking about it for a long time now, thinking in confused, obscure, obsessive, contradictory images about Pierre and about the path that leads back to the totality of things. But I never regretted leaving that place. I was glad I left, glad I left Pierre behind and came back alone, though this was something I found impossible to explain to anyone who didn't know Oneiros. I also found it hard to explain to myself. Perhaps my failure to understand it was a measure of my ignorance of Oneiros itself. That's why I've had to write everything down, struggling to make sense of it. And now I believe I understand.

I imagine Oneiros will always be somewhere near me from now on. Something will happen and I'll hear that music again, remember how I left Pierre and the site behind, and sadness will overwhelm me, for in leaving I made two farewells. Abandoning Pierre was one of them, abandoning the place itself was the other. And yet I don't think I will ever come to feel I should have stayed. I've been over it all so many times now and have never thought that was the road I should have taken. What I did was right and I'm glad I did it.

But my departure from this clinic is another thing. I still don't see myself handing this account to the doctor, thereby declaring myself cured and leaving by the main entrance, as it were. I'm more likely to say nothing and leave by a side door. There's no longer any reason for me to stay, but I still want to spend some time as hidden away as I can be from other people's eyes. So I shall just make one clean copy of this text and leave it on the doctor's desk when I go, in case they get worried and come looking for me. Then I shall take occasional simple jobs that don't require me to talk much to other people, and wander here and there around the country. That's how I'll live.

The music has started again. I look back, I walk the stony road, I hear the voices singing; then it stops and I become myself again. I suppose this is how I may learn to forget Oneiros one day, simply by having this experience over and over again, hundreds and hundreds of times, until I have built an Oneiros within me, whose music I will keep on hearing in my subconscious mind. While my ordinary, everyday life goes on, I'll be remembering that far-off place, thinking of it twenty-four hours a day, even though I will have forgotten it. I look forward to that day.

But now I hear the sounds again. I hear them quite clearly. I can still hear them ... hear them ...